Her house had been destroyed!

Her mind clicked like a telegraph through what would have to be replaced. The television, the carpet, the curtains that hung half off their rods...

The curtains.

April froze, her eyes narrowing. She looked at the police officer next to her. "Did you close the drapes?"

He shook his head, and Daniel gestured toward the window. "Open them."

Picking his way through the shards of April's life, the man fumbled through the ripped cloth for the cord, then slowly drew back the drapes.

At the sight of the windows, Daniel gasped out a low, choked prayer. "Dear God, save us."

April's eyes widened as her breath left her. She stumbled back against Daniel, who braced her, his hands closing on her shoulders.

The block letters trailed across the glass in smeared reddish-bronze lipstick, and the splintered tubes clustered beneath the window, crushed into the carpet.

The message was simple.

YOU TALK

YOU DIE

Books by Ramona Richards

Love Inspired Suspense

A Murder Among Friends
The Face of Deceit
The Taking of Carly Bradford
Field of Danger

RAMONA RICHARDS

A writer and editor since 1975, Ramona Richards has worked on staff with a number of publishers. Ramona has also freelanced with more than twenty magazine and book publishers and has won awards for both her fiction and nonfiction. She's written everything from sales-training video scripts to book reviews, and her latest articles have appeared in *Today's Christian Woman, College Bound* and *Special Ed Today.* She sold a story about her daughter to *Chicken Soup for the Caregiver's Soul,* and *Secrets of Confidence,* a book of devotionals, is available from Barbour Publishing.

In 2004, the God Allows U-Turns Foundation, in conjunction with the Advanced Writers and Speakers Association (AWSA), chose Ramona for their "Strength of Choice" award, and in 2003, AWSA nominated Ramona for Best Fiction Editor of the Year. The Evangelical Press Association presented her with an award for reporting in 2003, and in 1989 she won the Bronze Award for Best Original Dramatic Screenplay at the Houston International Film Festival. A member of the American Christian Fiction Writers and the Romance Writers of America, she has five other novels complete or in development.

FIELD of DANGER

Ramona Richards

Steeple
Hill®

Published by Steeple Hill Books™

STEEPLE HILL BOOKS

Steeple
Hill®

Recycling programs
for this product may
not exist in your area.

ISBN-13: 978-0-373-44366-6

FIELD OF DANGER

Printed in U.S.A.

For God hath not given us the spirit of fear;
but of power, and of love, and of a sound mind.
—*2 Timothy* 1:7

To Phyllis, for all your advice and love.

I didn't choose you as Rachel's co-conservator;
God did. I'm just the grateful one.

ONE

When the shotgun went off, April Presley dropped her thermos and screamed.

Hearing her own scream scared her almost as much as the man with the gun did, and April clamped both hands over her mouth as she watched her next-door neighbor, Levon Rivers, crumple in the middle of the newly plowed section of his field. Levon and his killer were almost fifty yards away, but even at that distance, April could see the blossom of red on Levon's chest and a cold brace of fear flooded through her.

Then another screech burst through her tightly clamped hands as the killer swung around toward her, his face a blurry mask to her dazed, bewildered eyes. Without hesitation, he lifted the gun and fired again.

April ran.

The morning had started out so peacefully.

As usual, April had spent her morning half on business and half on enjoying the luscious garden of flowers, herbs and vegetables behind her cottage. Since moving to the tiny town of Caralinda, Tennessee, April had found solace and a kind of spiritual comfort in her gardening. Levon, whose cornfield ran right up to the edge of April's yard, had given her tips that had turned the wimpy cluster of plants into a thriving garden that filled the morning air with the scent of roses, lavender, sage, fuchsia, rosemary and a whole forest of day lilies.

In turn, April brought Levon a thermos of cold lemonade every day that he worked in the field. The sound of his tractor or truck thumping down the field road that ran alongside her house was her cue. Around ten in the morning, she'd wend her way through his cornfield to wherever he worked. Lemonade in the mornings was her token of thanks, and delivering it was usually much more of a joy than a chore.

Yet today, she had barely stepped from between the dense rows of stalks when the shot rang out, her gesture of friendship suddenly putting her in the line of fire. April fled, grateful for high summer and a corn patch thick enough to hide her, grateful that she had walked this field enough with Levon to keep her footing among the dry ruts and clumps of earth. She knew how to keep her head low and her arms out to push away the sharp green blades that slapped around her as she ran.

She was especially grateful that a shotgun had a limited range.

All these things helped her evade the killer, and April could hear his grunts of frustration as he tried to catch her through the corn, then heard the blast that did little but rain shotgun pellets harmlessly over the field. Finally April stopped, holding her sides and trying to catch her breath. She couldn't run any farther. She'd have to take her chances with staying hidden. She could still hear him stomping about, raging through the corn, the noise growing closer, then moving away, constantly demanding that she show herself. She could stay hidden a long time in Levon's expansive field, especially if the killer kept making a racket covering the sounds of her own movements as she slipped out of his path. But April knew if someone didn't come, he'd continue to search. And eventually find her.

April's knees buckled, and she dropped to the ground. Adrenaline and fear fogged her mind and made her arms and legs tremble uncontrollably. She needed to rest, make a plan. *Calm down, girl. Lord, I need Your help. Guide me out of this. Show me what I need to do.* She drew her knees to her chest and hugged them to her, trying to still her quivering limbs. If she could only get home, call for help. But she'd gotten so turned around she knew she wouldn't be able to find the path without standing up fully to get her bearings…and putting herself back in the killer's sight. How would she get out of the field without the killer seeing her? And had he seen her well enough to know who she was?

These questions echoed in her mind. Her muscle tremors quieted, but her thoughts still swirled out of control, pushing her close to panic. She fought to sit still, to focus.

Normally the smell of the ripening corn and tangy scent of the leaves refreshed her. Today, they were oppressive. The hard-packed earth absorbed the sun while the dense rows of corn blocked most of the wind. April felt as if she were sitting in an oven. Her stomach growled, and she held her breath, waiting to see if the killer had heard it. *What do I do now?*

He hadn't. The killer's calls actually lessened as he moved farther away. But she could still hear him, his actions muffled by the plants and the stifling air of midday. April dared to stand up just enough to get her position, then ducked back down and closed her eyes, trying to plan. Her home and Levon's bordered a field road south of these acres of corn, but the shooter still prowled between her and those points of safety. To the east lay the open field where the shooting had occurred and west of her, a narrow country road wandered through the landscape. The open land in both of those directions could easily put her into direct contact or line of sight with the killer, with no place to hide. *Not a good idea.*

North? April opened her eyes. Now that direction held a glimmer of hope. Just beyond the cornfield...

Soft footsteps padded in the dirt behind her, and April spun around, her heart almost stopping with fear. An old woman stood there, her long white hair held down by a wide-brimmed straw hat and her finger pressed to her lips, indicating that April should remain silent. Beside her, a white German shepherd stood, head held low and pressed against the woman's hip.

Gulping air in relief, April nodded, and the woman motioned for her to follow her. Moving slowly, the three of them headed north, and April's hope bloomed as her panic faded enough for her to realize exactly who she followed.

Everyone in Caralinda called Lucretia Stockard "Aunt Suke," but April hadn't yet been able to find out why. And, at this moment, she cared very little about the odd nickname. All that mattered was the woman's house, just past the northern corner of Levon's property. She followed Aunt Suke's careful, silent footsteps as they moved slowly toward the edge of the field. At the end of the row, Aunt Suke paused and turned her head, listening. The dog stood still, head tilted to watch Aunt Suke, waiting for her command. The angry shouts had stopped, but April could still hear the sound of cornstalks being slashed aside not too far away and rapidly coming closer. Aunt Suke took one step forward, looked left and right, then motioned for April to come up next to her.

They were standing at the edge of Aunt Suke's backyard. The soft expanse of dark green grass led right to the back of the brick antebellum Stockard mansion. At the back of the house, slanted double doors leading to a root cellar stood open, their white slats gleaming in the summer sun.

Aunt Suke pointed at the root cellar and said one word. "Run."

April fled toward the safety of the 170-year-old house, even though the yard felt as if it were the size of a football field. Out of the corners of her eyes, she could see Aunt Suke and the dog running alongside her. As the three neared the doors, she heard a rage-filled roar echo over the field. He'd seen them, and even as Aunt Suke shoved her hard down the stone steps into the cellar and slammed the doors, April knew the planks of wood wouldn't hold against the killer's rage.

With a movement made familiar by years of living in the giant home, Aunt Suke slid a wooden bar through the handles of the cellar doors and swung around, eyes bright with command. "Polly!" Her voice snapped the word out in a harsh whisper. "Upstairs! And stay!"

April watched as the white shepherd turned toward a set of steps to the left of the doors and trotted upward. Aunt Suke then motioned April to the right, where a trapdoor was barely visible in the shadows. Aunt Suke hustled her down the ladder and followed quickly behind her into the pitch-dark room.

The older woman pulled the door shut, just as the first blast of the shotgun thundered against the cellar doors.

Daniel Rivers refused to believe what he'd heard over the radio. The county dispatcher who took the 911 call apparently did believe it, however, and her usually dispassionate voice shook as she alerted the units. Daniel stared at the radio a moment. This had to be a prank. Or he'd not heard it right.

Why would there be a shooting at Dad's?

He picked up the radio mike. "Unit A12. Base, repeat the call."

Silence followed, then his cell phone rang. He checked the number. It was the station. His fingers trembled a bit when he answered. "Rivers."

Martha Williams had been a dispatcher for the Bell County sheriff's department for almost forty years, and her nasal, drawling voice normally was as steady as a low river on a hot day. Now the voice shook with shock. "Daniel, it's true. The 911 call came from Aunt Suke. She says someone shot Levon and is trying to shoot April Presley."

Ice formed in Daniel's gut, and the images of his father and April Presley flashed through his mind. His father's face, leathery and creased from long years of hot sun and bright laughter, brought forth memories of their last fight, just a few days ago. Daniel loved his dad, but their relationship had evolved into what Daniel thought of as "civil animosity."

April, on the other hand... "April," Daniel whispered. From the moment he'd met her at one of his dad's infamous barbecues, Daniel had responded to her as he had no other woman. His chest tightened whenever she came near him, and the urge to hold her close and protect her surged through him.

She'd been gentle as she had turned down his invitation to dinner, explaining that it was too soon after her divorce. Daniel knew he should have moved on to other women, but he couldn't. In his heart he knew April was the one he was supposed to wait for.

Now he just hoped he hadn't waited too long.

"This has to be wrong." He cleared his throat.

"Aunt Suke's getting on in years. Her eyes aren't as sharp as they used to be. Maybe…maybe there's been a mistake."

"Maybe. The sheriff is on his way, though, to check it out."

Daniel reached to start the engine on his patrol cruiser. "I am, too. Thanks, Martha."

"Be careful, baby."

"You know I will." Daniel dropped the phone and gravel spun as he slid the car into a U-turn away from the speed trap he'd been watching and toward his father's farm. He hit the siren, which screamed as the cruiser raced down the road. Daniel pushed it hard through the curves of roads he'd driven since he was fifteen.

He didn't want to think about what Martha had said. It had to be wrong. Why would anyone want to shoot his father or April? Everyone in town loved Levon, and April— No, he couldn't even stand the thought of anyone hurting April. He pressed down harder on the accelerator. He'd be there soon, and then he'd see that this was all just a big mistake.

Suke Stockard was wrong. She *had* to be wrong.

"Please, Lord," Daniel whispered under his breath. "Please let her be wrong."

April flinched as the killer crashed into the cellar, the wooden door splintering under his assault. Aunt Suke clutched her arm, pressing her harder against the gritty wall at their backs. The room, pitch-black as any cave, smelled sour and acidic, like old dough, potatoes, onions and garlic. The taste in her mouth was acidic, too—a mix of adrenaline and fear.

"April Presley!" The killer's voice sounded flat and cold and far too close. "You can't hide forever. You, too, Suke Stockard. I *will* kill you."

Upstairs, Polly set up a raucous series of barks and yelps, and they could hear her running through the rooms.

A second blast from the gun made both women jump, and April bit her fist to keep from screaming. Terror clenched tight around her, making her shake.

Aunt Suke slid an arm around her, pulling her tight against her. Her thin limbs were wiry with tense muscles, and April wished she could draw in some of the older woman's strength. She inhaled deeply, trying to remain still and silent, not daring to relax, even as they heard his footsteps on the stairs, hard thumps headed upward.

Then another sound reached April, one that made her heart leap for joy. Police sirens.

The killer heard them, as well. "This ain't over!" His hoarse, raspy voice echoed through the house as he ascended the stairs and headed toward the backyard. "The cops can't protect you. Before this day is out, you're both dead!"

TWO

Daniel skidded the car into the familiar driveway, then turned down the field road that ran along the edge of the corn, toward the police lights he could see flashing up ahead. A cluster of emergency vehicles circled the crime scene, and he stopped the cruiser near the sheriff's car. He got out, still denying the growing dread in his heart.

When Daniel saw the strained horror in Sheriff Ray Taylor's face, however, he knew there had been no mistake. Then he spotted the blue tarp over the body on the ground, and plunged toward it with a gasp of pain. It took Ray and two other deputies to stop him, and he shoved back hard, his shoes digging into the dirt and scuffing backward as he pushed. "Let me see him!"

Ray blocked his way. "Daniel! Listen! I'm not going to keep you from seeing him, but you have to listen first. Look at me!"

Daniel stopped pushing against the older man, but couldn't seem to take his eyes off the blue tarp until Ray repeated the command with all the power of his Marine training. "Rivers, look at me!"

Daniel did, and Ray's voice softened. "Your father

took a shotgun blast to the chest at close range. Probably 12-gauge, from the look of it. It's not something you really want to see, and I don't care what you saw on the streets of Nashville. This is your father."

Daniel felt like a block of ice, numb and distant. "I have to see him."

Ray nodded. "We've cleared a spot so the coroner can get to him without messing up any evidence. There are footprints we still have to cast. I'll take you."

With Ray's hand on his shoulder as comfort and guide, Daniel stepped toward the tarp slowly, hard clumps of the plowed ground popping into dust as he trod on them. Everyone around him fell totally silent. Only Ray and Daniel approached the body, Ray bending to pull back the tarp, uncovering Levon's face.

Daniel dropped to his knees next to his father, his eyes burning. Levon's face, gray and speckled with brownish-red drops, seemed oddly peaceful. It had been a long time since Daniel had seen that kind of calm, that kind of peacefulness on his father's face—not since his mother had died five years ago. In that instant, Daniel felt a strange sense of comfort, and he knew, without a doubt, that his father was with God—and his mother.

"Tell her I still love her." The words came out in a choked rasp, then Daniel gave in to his own racking grief.

April wrapped her hands around a cold glass of tangy iced tea, twisting the glass round and round on the table, still not able to drink. Her hands still shook too hard to pick up the glass. From her position at the large oak table in Aunt Suke's kitchen, she could hear the fading voices at the front of the house, but couldn't make out what was being said. It was just as well; she didn't really want to know. The sturdy table and solid chair beneath her felt unmovable, even though April's world still spun around her.

She barely noticed when the young officer who had come in response to Aunt Suke's second 911 call left, the front door closing firmly behind him. Just moments before he had sat here at this table, holding April's hand and reassuring her that the sheriff's team would find the killer. He'd taken a preliminary statement from her, and while he'd tried to be kind and tactful, he had confirmed what April already knew in her heart.

Levon was dead. He had not just been wounded or knocked out. The close-range shot had taken the life of her friend. More than a friend, she thought, tears stinging her eyes. Levon had been like family to April since she'd moved to Caralinda almost a year ago, eager to be away from city life and her crazed former in-laws down in Nashville. Just last week, he had repaired a broken window at her house—one of many things he'd helped her with over the past year.

More than a friend. Almost a father. Certainly better than her own father had been.

April closed her eyes and tears leaked down her cheeks. *What now, Lord? What's next? He wants to kill me. What do I do?*

A mix of denial and anger settled over Daniel. His mind swirled with questions and wild speculations, even as his body felt remote, distant from him. He leaned against the fender of his cruiser, arms crossed, watching as his fellow officers hovered just outside the crime scene while the Bell County Coroner examined the body of Levon Rivers. Since Daniel was the victim's son, Ray had banned him from the site and the investigation, but Ray couldn't force him to leave, even though he had insisted that Daniel go home and start doing whatever it is you do to bury your father.

Somewhere in the back of his mind, the thought "It's not real. He's not dead" hovered, trying to break through. He wanted to let it, to wake up from this nightmare occurring in the bright July sun. Wake up and see Levon standing there, laughing at them for their worry.

Instead the officers kept working. Scouring the ground for evidence—marking footprints, blood spatter, stray buckshot pellets. The blue tarp had been pulled away as the coroner worked, and now one of her assistants stood by with a black body bag. In his years as a cop, Daniel had seen a lot of body bags, but somehow the grief associated with them had never struck home. Not like this.

Lord, what am I going to do?

Behind him, the telltale crunch of tires on gravel warned him of another car's arrival, and he turned slightly to see Deputy Jeff Gage get out of a cruiser and motion for Ray. Ray approached, one look at Daniel telling him to stay put. He and Gage met in the driveway several yards away from Daniel.

Gage, tall and lanky, moved with the grace of the long-distance runner he was. A gentle man who seemed barely tough enough to be a cop, Gage had a voice made for an unamplified stage. No matter how softly he spoke, his voice carried.

So Daniel had no trouble hearing Gage's report to Ray about his visit to Suke Stockard's.

"Talk to me," Ray said.

Gage shook his head. "Not good. April is holed up

at Aunt Suke's but says she never saw the shooter's face. His back was to her, then she ran. Can't blame her for not looking back. The guy blew the back door off the cellar over there, put a couple of holes in the floor, looking for her and Aunt Suke. Claims he'll kill them."

Ray growled. "Probably to keep them quiet."

"Looks like."

"Does he know who she is?"

Gage nodded. "He called her by name."

"You left them alone?"

Gage shook his head. "New guy in a car out front. Another at the back. Knew it would be the secondary crime scene. Should be enough to keep the guy away, at least until dark."

Ray nodded. "Good. Get over to April's house and make sure it's secure. We're about done here. When we are, I'll get her to the station for a complete statement and we'll take a look at that basement. Then we'll decide what to do to keep her safe."

The sheriff tapped Gage on the shoulder, and the lanky deputy started toward the crime scene. Ray hesitated, then came to Daniel. His face was stern, but his voice held the gentleness of a coach talking to an injured player. Ray Taylor was young for a sheriff, still in his thirties, but he was a widower as well as a former Marine officer, and wise beyond his years. "Rivers, go home. Call your family."

Daniel shook his head. "I can't. I need to be—"

"No. You can't be a part of this, Rivers. You *know* that."

"Ray—"

The sheriff's voice dropped in tone again as he interrupted. "Daniel, listen to me. You can*not* be here. You need to call your family, take care of arrangements.

Let us do our jobs. This is a time for you to be his son, not a cop. You stick to the details, all the things that have to be done. They'll get you through it."

Daniel started to protest again, but the expression on Ray's face told him that his widowed boss spoke from personal experience and wouldn't budge on this point. Finally he nodded and rubbed a hand over a face swollen by grief. "I don't even know where to start."

"The calls. Make one to Beck's Funeral Home. They'll walk you through it."

Daniel pushed away from the car and reached for the driver's door. "But you'll keep me updated, right?"

"Like we would any family. I promise."

Daniel got in the car and backed it out of the driveway, aware that Ray kept his eyes on him until the car was out of sight. He knew Ray didn't quite trust him to just give up and go home to sit with the phone.

Ray knew him well.

A hundred yards from the field path, the corn ran right up to the road, with only a few feet separating the stalks from the pavement. Daniel pulled off into the dirt there, out of sight, and cut the engine of the cruiser. Gripping the wheel with both hands, he squeezed as hard as he could, straining every muscle in his arms and body, desperate to drive the numbness away, to find the anger again.

His father. Levon. Dad. A low growl grew from deep in his gut, expanding into a rage-filled roar that filled the car, which rocked as he shook the wheel furiously. Daniel's eyes burned and his throat turned raw as the wrath slowly passed, leaving him feeling empty again, as if part of his soul had been ripped away.

Daniel breathed deeply as dozens of images flashed

through his mind, in rapid succession. His father on his tractor, in the backyard garden, stretched out in his recliner with the television remote slipping from his hands as he fell asleep. Levon in church, his face beaming whenever Daniel sang a solo from the choir loft.

Levon Rivers, born in North Carolina to a Native American mother and white father, had one of the most expressive faces Daniel had ever seen, and all his emotions shone through. Anguish over his wife's death, joy over a good baseball game, melancholy over memories, serenity over the comfort he took in his faith. The thought of his father cold, still and silent seemed so wrong.

Levon always spoke his mind. So did Daniel, which had led to legendary fights between father and son. The disappointment over Daniel's decision to become a cop instead of a farmer had echoed between them, fueling arguments for years. Although Levon had finally grown proud of his son's work, their relationship had felt the strain. Daniel knew he and his father hadn't been as close as they could have been—as close as Levon had wanted them to be.

Levon adored his family, took pride in his town, cherished his friends. His annual weekend-long barbecue emphasized all of that. Levon loved having people over, and at the last barbecue, he had seemed intent on introducing April Presley to everyone in Caralinda.

April. She'd been here almost a year, but had kept mostly to herself. They'd talked, usually at Levon's, but he didn't really know her. Gage had said she'd witnessed the shooting, then been chased and threatened by the gunman, but he hadn't said if she was hurt.

And physical injury aside, Daniel knew April had to

be traumatized. Levon had been a good friend to her and no one should have to watch a friend die like that. Daniel knew *that* firsthand. Jeff Gage's youth could work against an interrogation if April had a traumatic memory block of some kind. He had only been a cop for a few years. Without experience, Gage could push her in the wrong direction, make her so frightened of her memories that she'd blank them out permanently.

"But I could help." Daniel had been with a number of witnesses to horrible crimes who could barely remember their own names at first. In Iraq. On the streets of Nashville. He should talk to her. Calm her down. Show her how to deal with her fear and pain. Make her feel safe again.

Daniel shook his head. No. Ray would have his hide if he talked to the primary witness.

But April was more than just a witness. And he couldn't stand the thought of abandoning her when he might be able to help her through her pain.

With that thought, the drive to see April strengthened. Giving in, Daniel reached for the keys. He'd help April deal with what she'd seen. And then, freed from fear, her memory would come back, allowing Daniel to catch his father's killer. She had to know more then she thought she did.

She had to.

Aunt Suke pushed a bowl full of fresh mint leaves toward April. "Have some. It'll help."

April reached for a leaf and twisted it several times, releasing the sweet scent and gentle oil, before dropping it into her iced-tea glass. "How did you know? I mean, what was happening in the field."

"I heard the shotgun blast when he killed Levon— that was what brought me to the window. And then I saw him chasing you, firing that gun." She waved her hand idly toward the kitchen's ceiling. "We have four floors here, counting the cellar. Sixteen-foot ceilings. And the house is on top of a rise in the ground. From the top, I can see all the way to Robertson County. I called 911, and then went to get you."

She paused, glancing with annoyance at a splintered hole in the floor near the stove. "Can't believe that wretched buzzard blew a hole in my floor."

"Just be glad it wasn't us." April frowned. "Why did you hide us downstairs?"

Aunt Suke cleared her throat. "He had to have known that I'd called the police, and that his time was running out. Folks in a hurry usually see only the obvious."

"The stairs."

"Right. That's why I sent Polly upstairs to make noise."

April glanced at the complacent dog lying on the floor beside the table. "Wouldn't that put her in danger?"

"Trust me. The shooter was in a lot more danger than Polly."

April shuddered. "He called my name."

"Hmm." Aunt Suke watched her a few more moments, then asked softly, "How close were you?"

April shook her head. "Not close. Like I told the officer, I couldn't see who shot Levon. He had his back to me. But I could see Levon, see the—" Her voice broke. "I can't." Her gaze focused on the wooden table that had been polished to a silky finish by years of use.

Aunt Suke sipped her tea. "The sheriff will be back here shortly to take us both to the station for our complete statements. They've started clearing the scene. You need to get ready to talk to them. Ray Taylor is a good man, but it'll be all business."

April frowned. "You sound like you've been through this before."

Aunt Suke pushed a long strand of white hair behind one ear. She usually let her hair hang freely, and April had often seen her working in the garden, the wind swirling her hair around her head like a cloud. Only on Sundays did she neatly contain it with a thick barrette clasped just below her neckline. "I may not get out much these days, but there still isn't much I don't know about how this town runs."

April smiled, and Aunt Suke joined her, reaching across the table to grasp one of April's hands. "That's better. You can't let this shake you to the core."

April heard the plaintiveness in her own voice. "I saw a man get killed!"

Aunt Suke tightened her grasp. "I know. It rips you. But you have to hold it together. They have to find out who did this. If you let it shake you, you won't be able to help them."

"I'm not sure I can anyway."

"You may know more than you realize." Aunt Suke suddenly stood. "You need some snicker doodles."

"Cookies?" April asked weakly.

Aunt Suke paused and looked at April steadily. "Trust me. It's going to be the normal, everyday things that get you through this. Cookies. Tea. Friends. Family. What about your sisters?"

"June's not back from that conference in California

yet. I haven't called her because I know she'd want to come home early, and she doesn't need to. She flies home next week." April sighed. "I love my sister, but to be honest, I don't know if I can handle June right now. She'll want to take over everything. Tell me what to do and tell Ray how to run the investigation."

"You don't think Ray could rein her in?"

April shook her head. "They're not close enough yet. He'd just irritate her."

"What about Lindsey?"

April paused, not really wanting to cross into this territory and talk about her other sister. "Lindsey and I aren't on good terms right now. We talk, but we're not what you'd call close. Besides, she's still at a culinary school in D.C." April shook her head. "No. I don't have many friends here in Caralinda. And I lost my closest friend today."

Raising an eyebrow, Aunt Suke reached out to clasp her hand. "Well, you found a new one, as well. Two, if you count Polly." After one last squeeze to April's hand, she stood.

As Aunt Suke went to the cookie jar, Polly perked up, and April looked around the industrial-size kitchen. High-ceilinged and filled with dark woods and polished bronze appliances, it was a practical combination of old and new. She sighed. There was such a romantic nature about a house this old and historic. Levon had spent many an hour talking about the Stockards when April first moved to town, especially the house, which was one of the oldest in Caralinda.

Levon had said…

April pushed the thought away and brushed another tear from her eye.

The plate of cinnamon-laced cookies added a pungent aroma to the air, and Aunt Suke tossed one to Polly, who caught it neatly with a powerful snap of her jaws. Aunt Suke sat, waving a hand at April. "Stop thinking about Levon and my house and eat a cookie."

April sighed. "How did you know?"

Aunt Suke shrugged. "You're going to have flashing thoughts about Levon for a long time to come. It's natural. Part of grieving. Part of the questioning. As time goes by, you'll want to think about anything but what happened in the field. Your mind will wander, especially to those normal things." She smiled. "As to the house...happens every time someone sees inside for the first time. When this is over, I'll give you a tour."

"I'd like that. I love old homes. I was raised in one. But you're right, the tour should wait until later, when my mind is clear again." April focused on her tea again. "I can't believe Levon is dead. He was a good friend. It just doesn't seem real."

"Which is why you're not grieving for him yet. You will. It'll be real all too soon."

The doorbell stopped April's reply, sending a long series of melodic gongs echoing through the house. Polly stood with a soft woof and bounded out of the kitchen. April flinched, almost involuntarily, and the two women looked at each other a moment.

Then Aunt Suke straightened an already stiffened spine. "Probably just the sheriff. That turkey buzzard murderer may be determined, but even he would have better sense than to just ring my doorbell."

Both stood and April followed Aunt Suke from the kitchen through the connecting rooms, down a hallway to the front of the house and into a long, elegant entrance foyer. Polly waited at the door as Aunt Suke looked through the peephole then unlocked and opened the massive oaken door to her home.

Daniel Rivers stepped inside without invitation, immediately spotting April. At the sight of the devastation on his face, Levon's death abruptly became real.

She took one step toward Daniel, then burst into tears.

THREE

Anger drained away from Daniel as he closed his arms around April's shoulders. His shoulders dropped as he held her, whispering into her hair. "I'm sorry. I know you loved him, too."

April pushed back and looked up at him, a tinge of red returning to her skin, brighter because the rest of her face remained so pale. She nodded and stepped away from him, looking away, her gaze suddenly distant. "Like a father."

Aunt Suke tugged at his arm, and Daniel looked down at her.

"Does Ray know you're here? He'll have your skin on his wall if he doesn't."

Daniel heard the truth in her words and looked down at April again, wishing she'd let him hold her, comfort her. *Comfort each other.* But April would not look at him, even though tears still streaked her face.

He focused on Aunt Suke. Her white hair spread out over her shoulders like a wide fan, and her blue eyes flared with the fire of a mother bear protecting her cub. "You shouldn't be here, Daniel. You can't make me believe Ray wants you working on this."

A spear of annoyance shot through Daniel, but she was right. Daniel had spent more than twenty years trying to figure out how Aunt Suke knew everything about everybody in town. Then, about ten years ago, he'd given up and accepted it as a fact of life in Caralinda.

Ray *would* have a fit if he knew Daniel had stopped at Aunt Suke's. Ray's strict instructions to stay away from the case and the scene had sound reasoning behind them. Not only would Daniel have no objectivity about the murder, but his involvement would be a perfect target for a defense attorney. Ray had told him to go home and start making calls to his family.

Except that he couldn't. He had to do *something,* and he knew that he could interrogate April with an experience almost everyone on the force except Ray lacked. Only, he hadn't exactly gotten off to a professional start. He should be asking questions. Instead, he wanted to hold her close and make the pain go away.

Daniel closed his eyes and inhaled deeply, trying to shove down the grief roiling inside. Letting the breath out slowly, he slid his hat off his head and ran one hand through his black hair.

"Sorry, Aunt Suke." He looked at the woman standing behind her. "My apologies, April. It's just that…well, Dad, he…" He stopped, trying to gather thoughts scattered to the winds by grief. "I knew you were here and that you saw…"

As his voice trailed off, Aunt Suke softened and reached for his arm. Polly, sensing the change in mood, relaxed and slowly wagged her tail. "Well, you're here now. Get out of the door and stop letting all my cold air out. Sit down in the front parlor and get yourself together." With small, affectionate prods, she ushered them all into the only room in a fifty-mile radius that could legitimately be called a "front parlor" and opened thick damask drapes to let in the bright sun.

Obviously a room for entertaining ladies, the elegant, spotless parlor had tall windows, a tasteful selection of Queen Anne furnishings and a soft, Oriental rug over a polished hardwood floor. The graceful, feminine room made Daniel a little nervous, and he immediately checked his shoes to see if he'd tracked anything in.

Aunt Suke caught the move, smiled and patted his arm. "Don't worry about it, honey. Today is not a day to worry about a little dirt. Sit."

He did, on a sofa that looked too fragile to hold his weight. But it felt solid beneath him, and he relaxed a little, watching as April perched uneasily on a small chair on the other side of a low coffee table, her tall, slender frame making the slightest of depressions on the cushion. She was avoiding eye contact. Was she embarrassed at the way she'd cried on his shoulder? He hoped not. He was *glad* that she'd felt she could turn to him for comfort. The only part that bothered him was how she'd pulled away when the tears finally stopped. He wouldn't have minded holding her a little longer.

"I'm sorry," she said. "I didn't mean to fall apart like that. I'm sure this must be hard enough for you without me making it worse. I'm just… I'm sorry about your dad." Her tight voice held a slight tremor. "He was a good man. A good friend. I wish I could help you find the man responsible. But I didn't really see…just the gun…and then I ran and hid in the corn."

As April's words faded, Aunt Suke sat next to Daniel and spoke softly to April. "You've been shook to the core, and who can blame you? There's no call to be apologizing for that."

Daniel looked down at the rug, sorrow and frustration tearing a hole in his entire being over his own loss, and what all of this was doing to April. He knew this was exactly why Ray had told him to go home; he had to get control of his feelings or he wouldn't be of any use to anyone.

He looked up again, this time meeting the uncertain look in April's bright green eyes dead-on. "I can help you with that."

"What?"

"I can help," he repeated to April. "I know how rough it is to see someone get shot. I know it disrupts everything you thought right and good. That anyone could turn a gun on another person just doesn't register with most of us, and that's the way it should be. And I know you're terrified."

"Not exactly."

He stopped, waiting for her to go on, watching as she took a deep breath and sat a bit straighter in the chair.

"I mean, I was with that man shoving his way through the corn, firing shots in the air, threatening me in the cellar—"

Daniel's eyes widened. "Did he call you by name or were the threats just wild?"

April looked very small and still in her chair. "He called my name. Said he would kill me." She swallowed hard. "Kill us. Said the cops couldn't protect us."

"He's wrong." Daniel leaned forward on his seat. "We can help you. *I* can help you. I know it's hard right now, with the shock and horror blurring your memories, but if we work together, I think I can help you identify the killer."

Silence covered the room a moment, then Aunt Suke spoke softly. "You mean this is someone we all know."

Slowly Daniel nodded. "This wasn't a robbery or a carjacking. The killer didn't take anything but my father's life. This was someone with a personal grudge, not to mention someone who knew Levon well enough to know where to find him. There's not a doubt in my mind—the killer's a local."

April took a deep, cleansing breath and let it out slowly. "I've not been here long enough to make many friends. Aside from my sister, I barely know anyone but Levon, and the people he'd introduced me to."

All her muscles seemed to tighten. "But Levon didn't have enemies, did he? He was a great man. Everyone loved him. How could anyone want or have a reason to do this?"

Good question. One Daniel had already been turning over in his mind a hundred times. Levon Rivers was not only a good man, he was a *beloved* man. Daniel had never heard an ill word against his father the entire time he was growing up, and when he'd thrown a sixtieth birthday barbecue for Levon four years ago, the entirety of Caralinda showed up.

Whoever the shooter was, he'd managed to keep his grudge against Levon well-hidden. Would he be as successful at hiding his guilt now that the crime was done? Daniel was afraid so, which made April's blocked memories even more important.

He had to try a different tactic.

Daniel put his hat on the sofa beside him and leaned farther forward, resting his elbows on his knees as he focused on her eyes. "I know that you took him lemonade every morning he worked in the fields. He told me. He loved that about you, said it made him feel remembered, especially when he was doing something on his own, no hired folks about."

Her eyes glistened a bit at this, and she nodded.

"So you were on the way this morning, walking through the field."

She nodded again. "Through the corn."

"He planted it pretty dense this year."

Again, she agreed. "A different hybrid he was trying. Harder walking than last year, but he said it would make the harvest easier, with the way the combines worked. But it allowed a lot of weeds to grow up in some places." She smiled slightly, as if remembering something. "Levon encouraged me to walk around the fields, to use the field road to make it easier, but it was still quicker to go through. I told him that the harder hiking was good for me, that I needed the exercise. He laughed."

I'm sure he did, thought Daniel. April stood almost as tall as his own six-foot height, and her lean, muscular frame reminded him of an Olympic athlete. She had been softer, less muscular when she'd arrived in Caralinda a year ago, a beautiful, vibrant woman he'd wanted very much to spend more time with.

He'd even asked her out, but she'd told him that her divorce still stung and she couldn't manage anything but friendship. He'd understood, sort of. He'd been through breakups, but nothing as serious as a divorce.

April had obviously been healed by Caralinda, however. The days in the sun, walking the fields with his father, and the work in her own garden had slimmed her down even more and made her skin glow. Her emerald-green eyes had always been bright against her reddish-brown hair and the freckles that splattered across her face, but now they gleamed as they met his focused gaze without flinching.

She knows what I'm doing, he realized. *Good.* He cleared his throat.

"Did you hear anything before you stepped out of the corn?"

April thought for a moment, then shook her head.

"What did you see first?"

She closed those emerald eyes, and her brow furrowed. "His back. The shooter's. Then your dad."

"Was he taller than Dad?"

April hesitated a moment, trying to remember. "N-no. I could still see the top of your dad's head." She held her hands about two feet apart. "But broader. I think."

"What was the shooter wearing?"

She hesitated. "Jeans. Dirty. Beat-up jeans. A light shirt. White…or pale blue. Maybe."

"Anything on his head?"

"A ball cap."

"What color?"

Another pause, then she shook her head.

"What did you see next?"

The furrows deepened. "I saw…" Her eyes, still shut, clenched tighter. "Levon stepped back so I saw his face, then there was the shot…." She stopped, and tears leaked from the corners of her eyes and slid down her cheeks.

April opened her eyes. "I can't remember anything after that. I just…ran."

Daniel pressed down hard on the frustration, the

grief that threatened to boil over in him once more, and his already taut muscles clenched harder from the effort. She'd been doing so well, was clearly trying so hard. He'd gotten his hopes up that the memories were returning on their own by sheer force of will. But now she looked crushed all over again, even the little bit that she'd remembered hurting her all over again.

Daniel turned to Aunt Suke. "You called 911. You saw it?"

Aunt Suke shook her head. "I heard the first shot. By the time I got to one of the windows, all I could see was Levon on the ground, and two people tearing through the cornfield. When I realized one of them was April, I knew she'd probably seen what went down. I told the operator, then went after her."

"Could you see the shooter?"

Aunt Suke wagged a hand toward the cornfield. "Nothing. By the time I got to the window, he was crashing around in the corn. All I could see was the barrel of the shotgun as he used it to push back the stalks."

"Did either of you see a vehicle on either of the side roads? A car or a—"

The gongs of Aunt Suke's doorbell, followed by a determined pounding on the door, interrupted him. Polly bolted for the door with a series of sharp barks.

"That's probably Ray," Aunt Suke said softly.

Daniel stood, nodding almost to himself. "I'll get it. Take whatever he has to say." He hoped Ray would understand why he had to do this.

The pounding sounded again, and Polly's barks increased in volume. Daniel headed for the door, hat in hand. He herded Polly aside and pulled open the ancient door, faced Ray and waited.

Ray Taylor stared at him, his jaw clamped so tight that the muscles in his cheeks twitched. He stared at Daniel a moment, glanced briefly at Aunt Suke and then looked at April, who had taken up a position just to Daniel's right. After a moment, Ray let out a long exhale, as much a snarl as a sigh, and looked back to Daniel. "Boy, if you don't beat all. I will deal with you later."

Ray's gaze turned again to April. "Right now, Ms. Presley, you need to come with us."

Alarm surged through Daniel at the sheriff's statement. "What's happened?"

Ray glared at him. "You need to go home."

April stepped forward and placed a firm hand on Daniel's arm. Whether she needed support or offered it, he wasn't quite sure. "Please, Sheriff. What's happened?"

Ray hesitated, obviously still perturbed with his disobedient deputy. He looked from her, to Daniel, then back, as if he'd made up his mind about something. "I sent an officer to secure your house, Ms. Presley. He just radioed to say there are signs that someone has broken in."

April's fingers closed viselike on Daniel's arm, and he felt her body sway toward him, once again needing the support he was more than happy to give.

FOUR

"I want him to come. *Please.*" April hated the pleading sound in her voice, but she had to make the sheriff understand.

They stood in Aunt Suke's driveway, Ray Taylor's hand still on the top of his cruiser's door, which he had opened for April. He had just ordered Daniel to go home. Again.

Ray growled under his breath. "Ms. Presley—" He stopped and took a deep breath as if to calm himself. "April. Listen, it's bad policy to have family involved in these things, even if he's a trained officer of the law. Bad for the case and good for any defense attorney."

April glanced quickly at Daniel, who waited silently, his body tense but still, his ebony eyes focused on her. April knew he had to be a little wary of what she would say. Which was understandable, since she'd held him at bay since her arrival in Caralinda. But he'd asked her out so soon after her divorce that she'd had no choice but to turn him down. At that point she would have been skittish around almost any man.

They had not been around each other much since, even though Levon had clearly been on a campaign to

get them together. He'd frequently given her updates
about events in Daniel's life, and suggested that Daniel
would make an excellent husband. At first Levon's
matchmaking had been awkward, but after a bit, April
had found it almost charming that he cared so deeply
for his only son.

Daniel was a good man, and it had felt beautifully
natural to lean on him, to cry on his shoulders. But she
didn't want to appear false or cloying at a time like this.
April took a deep breath, searching for the words that
would tell Ray how much she needed Daniel to be
involved without sounding disingenuous. After all,
Daniel wasn't just a deputy sheriff in those moments;
he also was a man devastated by his father's murder, the
son of the only real friend she'd made in Caralinda
over the past year. And right now they *both* needed a
friend.

"I understand that, Sheriff, but your deputy is also
my friend. And right now I could use one with me."

Daniel's left eyebrow twitched, but he otherwise
showed no reaction.

Ray Taylor snarled and turned his back as he
returned to the driver's side of the cruiser. "All right, get
in, the both of you. You in front, April."

Daniel held the door for her, then shut it as she
buckled the seat belt. He got in behind her, and Ray
turned the car out of Aunt Suke's driveway and headed
toward April's house.

"What did Gage find?" Daniel asked.

Ray glanced in the rearview mirror. "When he found
the front door open, he called for backup, and I sent two
more officers over. The suspect has apparently been in
the house, but it's clear now."

April clutched her hands together in her lap, suddenly aware of how cold they were. "Did he say how bad it was?"

Ray hesitated, then shook his head once.

He knows. It must be awful. April straightened in the seat, trying to steel herself to see what had happened to her beloved cottage. They drove the rest of the short distance in silence, and as the cruiser bumped and rolled slowly up April's rough gravel driveway, she tried not to hyperventilate. She focused on Jeff Gage, noticing that he seemed anxious. She exhaled slowly, making herself sit still a moment. This, after all, was not her first break-in. Her parents' house had been burglarized when she was a teenager, and her first home had been broken into not long after her wedding. In both cases, the thefts had been quick and dirty, removing electronics, guns and, in the second robbery, all her wedding gifts. *You've been through this before. You know what it's like. You'll get through it again. Stay calm.*

Ray parked the car, and they got out, walking slowly toward the steps leading up to the porch. April stood at the foot of them, staring at the open door of her home, an odd hollow feeling growing in her chest. Her breaths came faster, and a slight dizziness settled over her.

Daniel stepped closer to her back, his warm presence reassuring her, as if she could lean back against him and never fall. "Are you okay?"

"Not yet," she whispered, and she knew they all watched her, waiting for her to react to the violation of her home.

Levon Rivers had built the small Cape Cod–style

cottage for his mother's sister, carving the plot from one corner of his expansive fields. When his aunt died, he'd rented it to a niece, who eventually decided to return to college. At that point, Levon had put the charming cottage on the market.

April, desperate to get out of Nashville and away from her hostile in-laws and bitter ex-husband, fell in love with it instantly and made an offer the first time she saw it. In the year since then, she'd polished the hardwood floors and painted everything in her beloved earth tones. She'd even picked out a new door made from heavy oak and featuring three long panes of beveled glass. All of her work had made it truly hers, secluded and cozy and loved.

Now someone had smashed open the door, shattering the glass and splintering the door frame.

Ray Taylor touched her arm. "I just want you to look around inside the door. Gage has already been in, so he's the only one I want moving around in the house. We will dust for prints later, so try not to touch anything. We need to know if you can tell if anything is missing."

April nodded, took a deep breath and climbed the steps. Stepping over the threshold, she braced herself for what she would see.

As she moved past the splintered front door, however, April saw that this was not just a burglary—this was a personal, vicious attack. As she scanned the room, her knees weakened, and she swayed, suddenly grateful for the firm strength of Daniel, who still stood close behind her.

His hand closed on her arm, steadying her. "You okay?" he asked again.

She nodded, not trusting her voice.

"You don't have to do this now."

She wrapped her fingers around his hand. "Yes, I do." The house held an echoing stillness that made her own home feel unfamiliar, as if she'd walked into the abode of a stranger. Forgetting Ray's instructions, she moved forward, her toes crunching down on a shattered cup.

She stopped, looking down. It wasn't the only dish on the floor. Her kitchen cabinet doors splayed wide, their shelves cleared of all contents. Broken china littered every open space on the floor. Cans of vegetables and soup rolled free, and flour, cereal and sugar dusted all surfaces while a faint scent of cornmeal and yeast hung in the air. Biting her lower lip, she scanned the room.

Destruction…yet nothing seemed to be missing. The television still stood in place, although its smashed screen looked like a dark star in a black hole. Not even everything had suffered. The CD player on one end table remained untouched, as did her collection of books and some of the CDs stacked neatly on one shelf of a bookcase. Other CDs were tossed about the room like confetti, their cases splintered. The randomness was nearly as disturbing as the violence. Her attacker had stood in her home and deliberately chosen which parts of her life to wreck, and which to keep intact.

"He didn't steal anything." April's voice sounded flat and hollow, even to her.

"Are you sure?" Ray asked behind them.

Before she could answer, Daniel whispered in her ear. "Is there anything really odd? Not the trashing. Something odd in the middle of it."

April felt a laugh borne of hysteria bubbling in the back of her throat, and she almost choked. Anything *odd?* Had he lost his mind? Her house had been destroyed! Her food, her fine china! *Her life!* Her gaze darted about the room as her mind clicked through what would have to be replaced. The television, the carpet, the curtains that hung half off their rods...

The curtains.

She froze, her eyes narrowing. The curtains on the back window were closed.

April blinked, her anxiety calming as she stared at the bright yellow and green fabric that added light and color to her open living room. Every morning, she opened both sets, on the front and back windows, to allow in as much light as possible. Now the ones on the rear window were closed.

April turned slightly toward the front window. Those curtains were still open.

She looked at Officer Gage. "Did you close the drapes?" She pointed at the torn fabric.

Confused, the young man looked from her to Ray.

The sheriff nodded. "Did you?"

Gage shook his head, and Ray gestured toward the window. "Open them."

Picking his way through the shards of April's life, Gage fumbled through the ripped cloth for the cord, then slowly drew back the drapes.

At the sight of the windows, Daniel gasped out a low, choked prayer. "Dear God, save us."

April's eyes widened as her breath left her. She stumbled back against Daniel, who braced her, his hands closing on her shoulders.

The block letters trailed across the glass in smeared

reddish-bronze lipstick, and the splintered tubes clustered beneath the window, crushed into the carpet.

The message was simple.

YOU TALK
YOU DIE

FIVE

Daniel recovered first. "He's wrong. I'm not about to let him hurt you. We *can* protect you." His voice, low and rumbling, held a worried edge to it, revealing the tight ball of grief that he worked to suppress. "But you have to let us help you. You may not remember him, but he definitely thinks you know who he is."

"But I don't!" April pushed away from Daniel and turned away from the wreckage. "I didn't see— He had this cap on—" She stopped, waving her hands vigorously in front of her, as if she could flick away the horrifying memory of Levon's murder. She clenched her jaw and growled through gritted teeth. "I did not see him!" Tears flooded her eyes and streamed from the outside corners as she turned to Ray. "I did *not* see him!"

The sheriff nodded solemnly. "I understand. We still need to get your statement, though, to get down everything you *did* see. You never know what might help."

April's shoulders dropped in acquiescence, then her eyes suddenly widened and she released a noise that sounded like a wounded animal. She swung around and fled toward a door at the far side of the kitchen. Daniel followed, despite Ray's bellowed protests at both of them.

April flung open the door, barely clearing it in her rush to get into the other room. Racing after her, Daniel almost collided with April as she abruptly stopped in the doorway, her gaze darting frenetically around as she examined every item in the room.

Daniel stared over her right shoulder. "What is all this?"

When Levon had built the house, the room had been a two-car garage. Now one half had been converted into a customized kitchen. Steel counters lined much of the wall space, broken up by a six-burner gas stove, restaurant-style sink and shelves laden with dozens of jars. A large refrigerator hummed against the far wall, and on one counter, empty and sparkling jars drained on thick cloths. Near the back of the room, bushel baskets full of an assortment of berries, fruits, corn and beans stood waiting, lacing the air with the sweet scent of fresh produce.

"Your business, right?"

April nodded, slowly approaching one set of shelves. "Levon helped me convert this space. Presley's Home Farm Organics." The shelf in front of her almost overflowed with finished product, the tightly sealed lids, crystal-cut jars and signature red and green labels representing hundreds of hours of work. She picked up one jar and examined the lid's seal. "Levon helped me create this recipe for black bean and corn salsa."

Daniel watched her, understanding the sorrow she must feel at each new reminder that her friend was gone. His throat tightened. "He learned to cook stuff like that when my mom got sick."

April's sad smile made him ache with a grief that threatened to roll over him again. "He did the taste testing and encouraging." She set the jar back on the shelf. "It's one of my bestsellers."

"Where do you sell it?"

April ran her finger along the shelf. "The Caralinda General Store carries it, and some of the places in White Hills. A few stores in Nashville. Mostly online. I've wanted to do this for a long time, but first my dad and then my ex always said I didn't have the head for it. No business sense. Said I'd fail." She paused, her voice softening. "Levon kept telling me I could do it. He believed in me."

She turned to Daniel, then the sheriff, who stood on the step down into the room. "The killer must have thought this was still the garage. Everything seems okay."

Both men looked around the room. All of the canning equipment and supplies did appear untouched. Even the polished concrete floor remained spotless.

Ray cleared his throat. "So although he knows who you are, where you live, he doesn't know about your business."

"Will that help?" April asked eagerly.

"Maybe. If we can be sure that that's the reason. It's possible he just ran out of time." Daniel pushed his shoulders back, fighting the stress-induced tension. This was the frustrating part of investigating—turning clues into theories…and then watching them fall apart.

April looked from one man to the other. "He chased us, Aunt Suke and me, right into the basement. He only left when we heard the sirens. She'll be in as much danger, won't she?"

"What was Aunt Suke—" Ray didn't quite get the words out.

"She saved me." April crossed to stand by Daniel's side, looking up at Ray. "She heard the shot, saw me running, then hiding. She came and got me. Her and that white dog."

"Polly," Daniel whispered.

"Polly."

Ray looked from her to Daniel a moment then back at April, as if contemplating his next move. "Are you sure nothing is missing here?"

At April's nod, Ray focused on his young deputy. "Go out that way." He pointed at a door at the back of the canning kitchen. "I don't want you going back through the house. I'm going to need Gage here. Pick up Aunt Suke and take them both back to the station and get their statements. *Don't* embellish, you hear me, Rivers?"

"Yes, sir."

"Then find them a place to stay, and you go home. Call whoever you need to. Understand?"

"No, sir."

Ray froze. "What did you say?"

Daniel straightened, not thrilled about standing up to his boss, even though he had to. "The killer knows who she is, Sheriff. There's no way she should be left alone. Even if Aunt Suke is with her."

Ray pursed his lips, face hard. Finally he relented. "Well, what do you have in mind?"

Daniel ignored the questioning look on April's face. "Someone needs to stay with her, make sure no one gets close. The minute we look away, he'll pull out that shotgun again. Wherever we put her, she needs to have one of us near."

Ray's eyes narrowed. "And you're volunteering. I told you that you need to stay away from this—"

"We're shorthanded right now, with two of the guys on vacation. You just said it. You need Gage here. You need everyone possible on this case. Guarding is not investigating."

Ray continued to watch him a moment longer, and Daniel knew all too well the insight Ray could hide behind narrowed eyes and tight lips. He'd learned long ago not to underestimate his ex-military officer of a boss, and he felt sure Ray knew exactly what Daniel hoped for.

That April would remember. That more time spent with her, talking through the trauma and helping her relax again would jog what she'd blocked from her conscious mind.

Daniel could almost see Ray's mind clicking through the list of his officers, evaluating skills and duties, to see if anyone could take Daniel's place. And he saw in the sheriff's eyes the moment Ray came to the conclusion that there was no one else.

Ray growled beneath his breath, then pointed at the door. "Get out, Deputy. Have someone take you back to your car and get her to the station. *Now!*"

"Yes, sir!" Daniel grabbed April's arm and pulled her toward the door.

Outside, she shook off his arm and turned to him, eyes narrow with anger. "What was *that* all about? I am not going into some type of hibernation, Daniel. I *won't*."

Daniel reached for her arm again, even as he waved for the attention of another officer. "Let's go before he changes his mind. I'll explain in the car."

They headed for the car, and Daniel opened the back door for her. He slid in next to her as the other officer got behind the wheel. "Take us back to Aunt Suke's."

Their driver nodded, and Daniel turned to face April, who spoke before he had a chance.

"I'm not hiding out somewhere, Daniel. Look, I spent a great deal of my marriage feeling terrified and isolated. He wanted to control every minute of my day. I'm not doing that again. I promised myself I'd no longer live in fear." She took a deep breath. "I'm serious, Daniel. I will not hide from this man. I'm never living like that again. Not even for a day."

He watched her closely, understanding her defiance, but also seeing the quiver in her fingertips and the uncertainty in her eyes. He reached for one of her hands, which was frigid, despite the heat of the day. He wrapped it in the warmth of both of his. "I know you want everything to just go back to the way it was. But that's not going to happen."

When she started to protest, he tightened his grip and kept talking. "For now, just listen to me. No, don't just listen. April, I need you to *hear* me." Daniel took a deep breath, pressing back the grief that hovered over his heart. "You saw my father get shot. Whether or not you recognized the shooter, he obviously saw you. I don't think he'll just trust that the threat he left on your window will keep you quiet."

"But I didn't see—"

"He doesn't know that. He doesn't know what you'll tell us. He doesn't know if you'll be terrified to speak or angry enough to tell us everything."

Her eyes widened as the truth really began to set in. "You really *do* think he'll come after me. Try to kill me."

Daniel nodded. "I *know* he will. He's killed already, and he won't hesitate to do it again. He confronted my father at the very time and place when no one should have been around, planning very carefully. He didn't expect to be seen. Your decision to bring Levon lemonade ruined his plans."

April closed her eyes a moment and pressed her other hand on top of his. Her voice was so low and hoarse that he could barely hear her over the noise of the cruiser. "Why would anyone kill your father? I just don't understand. He was the kindest man on the planet!"

Daniel's jaw tightened. "I don't know. But like with you and your house, this is someone who knew my father, knew when Dad would be in the field."

"So he's definitely local."

Daniel didn't like saying it, but he had to. "Yes. This is someone close, someone we may even see in church on Sunday."

April paled even more. "And you think he'll kill me the first time he finds me alone."

He nodded. "I think that's a real possibility. And since it's someone you may have seen around Caralinda, you won't even know who to be wary of. You can't trust anyone."

Her lips became a fine line. "Even you."

It was a challenge, but he met her stare squarely. "Even me."

She relented, her body sagging a bit. "Except that you would have a scream out with Levon, not a shooting."

It broke the tension of the moment, and Daniel almost laughed with relief. April had only been in Caralinda a year, but she'd been witness to more than a few of his fights with his dad. "You did get to see some of that, didn't you?"

Both of them had been temperamental and stubborn, both opinionated and perfectly capable of expressing those opinions at full volume. They'd fought about Daniel's career, his relationships, the farm, politics, religion, even money. Eventually, they'd realized that giving each other space was the easiest way to keep the peace. Daniel had been on his own since he was eighteen, but he'd always come back for Sundays and all holidays.

April nodded. "Good men with good opinions are going to fight sometimes." She shrugged one shoulder. "My dad and I never did. Or at least I never fought back." She let out a long, slow breath that seemed to deflate her. "Levon was the better father. Now he's gone, too."

Daniel wanted to ask what had happened between her and her father, but there wasn't time as the car pulled up in Aunt Suke's short driveway. "We're here." He held her elbow as she slid out of the backseat. "Watch your head."

Aunt Suke waited for them on the front porch, Polly pressed against her hip. She and the dog reached them quickly as the other car backed out and headed toward April's house again.

"I want to talk to you two. Now."

Daniel held up his hand. "I need to get you and April to the station to get your—"

"*Now.*" Aunt Suke's eyes, bright and wide with determination, left no room for argument.

Daniel bit back his protest, his impulse to act like a cop and take over the situation. Not even noon yet, but the exhaustion of grief and stress had settled a weariness in his muscles. "What about?"

Aunt Suke reached for April's hands. "I'm sorry about your home. I hope he didn't do too much damage."

Daniel scowled. "How did you—" He stopped. It didn't matter how. Aunt Suke always knew.

Aunt Suke continued to focus on April. "Clearly you can't go back there. You know you can't stay alone. Not till they catch him."

"I know, but—"

"We're already looking into places you both might—"

"We'll stay here."

Silence. April looked at Daniel, who shook his head, even though he knew arguing with Aunt Suke had always been a losing battle. "No, Aunt Suke. You could be in danger, as well. We can't guarantee your safety in a house this big, this open." He gestured around at the rolling fields that surrounded the house.

As if she understood, Polly tilted her head to look at Daniel, then Aunt Suke, whose spine stiffened. "I've not been afraid of any man since I was a nurse in Korea in 1951. If enemy artillery didn't frighten me, a coward with a shotgun is not even in the running."

"The sheriff won't—"

"Ray Taylor will listen to reason even if you won't. This big old house is safer than any chintzy motel out on the interstate, even with you sitting in front of the door. Lots of hiding places, and that's providing he gets in and Polly doesn't get him. You know what she can do."

Daniel ignored April's questioning look at Polly. Only Aunt Suke would bring a retired K-9 unit dog into her home. But retired or not, no one messed with Polly.

Or Aunt Suke, for that matter.

Hands on hips, Aunt Suke braced for battle, her

white hair swirling in a sudden breeze. "I have Polly. I have a house with an alarm system and a lot of hiding places. I'm sure April has a cell phone. And that's before you put a deputy in my driveway."

"No gun?"

Aunt Suke's mouth twisted in disgust. "Of course I have a gun, but I don't go around shooting at people, including your suspect."

"No shooting would be preferable, yes. What kind?"

"A shotgun I inherited from my father. It's clean, it fires fine, it's unloaded and it's in my bedroom closet. I use it to scare blackbirds and juvenile delinquents trying to smoke pot in my cornfield."

Daniel's eyebrows arched. Surely she wasn't ser—

Aunt Suke crossed her arms. "Daniel. I said I do not shoot at anyone. You're not thinking straight or you'd have caught that."

Daniel rubbed his hand hard across his mouth and turned away to look out over the cornfield that stretched away over the rolling ground next to the Stockard home. The cornfield where his father had died.

Grief threatened to close off his throat and Daniel's fists tightened, his nails digging into his palms as the sight of his father's gray face flashed in his mind.

A soft hand closed on his arm. "Daniel?"

Focus. *You're the guardian here. Lord, I need Your strength.*

Daniel looked down into April's intense green eyes, which widened with concern as she spoke. "I know you're worried about us staying here. It's dangerous. But you also know she's probably right. Not to mention that you're going to have a lot to do besides watching out for us every minute. You know you'll worry less if

I'm here with Polly and an alarm system rather than at a motel."

She gave his arm a gentle squeeze, then dropped her hand away. "Besides, you're the one who told me that Caralinda was like Mayberry most days—you usually put people over rules."

Daniel hesitated, wondering how she'd managed to see into his heart. Her words about considering people over the rules were so close to his exact thoughts, he felt she'd read his mind.

He took a deep breath. "On the other hand, I don't exactly work for Sheriff *Andy* Taylor. Ray's ex-military."

"But he's still a Southern good ole boy. The kind that goes to church on Sunday, takes good care of his mama and still tears up whenever 'The Star Spangled Banner' is sung. Do you really think he'd put rules over the wisdom of a woman his mother's age?" She tilted her head toward Aunt Suke. "I think she has that part pegged."

Daniel touched her shoulder. "But are you okay with this?"

April nodded. "We'll be fine. At least I'll have someone to talk to."

Giving in, Daniel cleared his throat and turned back to Aunt Suke. "I still have to take y'all to the station to take your statements. If Ray agrees to let you stay here, we'll secure the house—" The radio on his belt interrupted them as Martha's sharp drawl spat out words that made them all go pale.

"All units respond. Shots fired. I repeat, shots fired." She rattled off the address, then added, "Get the lead out, folks. He's got them penned down."

Daniel sprang for the car, ordering her to stay with

Aunt Suke. The two other officers guarding the house raced to their cruiser, ready to pull out behind him. Daniel slammed the car door, barely hearing April's last words.

"That's my house."

SIX

"That's my house," April repeated, wondering exactly how many shocks she'd have to live through today.

Aunt Suke reached for April's elbow. "It could also be a diversionary tactic. Let's get inside." She spoke to the white shepherd as they reached the porch. "Rounds, Polly."

Without missing a step, the dog turned and headed for the edge of the yard.

"Where's she going?"

Aunt Suke guided April inside, then closed and bolted the door. "She'll circle the yard to see if anything is out of place. Polly will sound an alert if she finds something."

"That's handy."

A wry smile crossed Aunt Suke's face as she went into the parlor, checked the locks on the windows and released the heavy drapes from their tiebacks. The room sank into a soft, almost comforting darkness as she spoke. "I've lived alone a long time, girl. A smart, well-trained dog is a better investment than mutual funds."

"What did you mean when you said, 'You know what she can do'?"

Aunt Suke checked the lock on the front door again, then the window locks and drapes in the music room opposite the parlor. "Polly used to be part of a K-9 unit. Her human partner was shot and killed in the line of duty, and Polly responded more viciously than the dogs are trained to do."

"She killed the shooter."

Aunt Suke paused, then nodded. "Afterward, they couldn't get her to reattach to another officer."

"But she bonded with you."

Aunt Suke returned to the foyer and motioned for April to follow her to the kitchen. "No explaining it. Maybe it was different because I was a woman. But they brought her here for me to take a look-see, and Polly got out of the car, circled the yard once, then came to stand by my side."

April trailed behind her. "Maybe she knew you needed her."

The older woman stopped and turned, her eyes glinting with humor. "Maybe she did at that. Never looked at it that way."

"At some level, we all want to be needed."

Aunt Suke's look turned somber as she appraised April a moment. "We do indeed. A wise statement from one so young."

"I'm thirty-two."

"And you won't realize until you're my age exactly how young thirty-two really is."

"What did you mean by 'it could be a diversionary tactic'?"

Aunt Suke turned and continued into the kitchen, speaking as she rounded the big room, closing curtains and double-checking the back door lock. "You heard

the dispatcher. Martha rallied the troops to your house.
That call will pull every officer off any current duty and
to that location."

"My house."

Aunt Suke paused and opened a tall, narrow pantry
door. She reached behind a spray of mops and brooms
and pulled out a wooden baseball bat, which she hefted
once. Carrying the bat, she checked the back door lock
and the door that led into the basement. "And I'm sorry
about that. Levon built a great little house, and from
what I hear, you really had it done up real cute."

April paused, leaning against one of the chairs and
looking down at the scarred table. "You should see it
now. He destroyed it."

"You couldn't have known you were walking into a
firefight this morning, girl. Now, come with me."

Like many antebellum homes, the Stockard mansion
had two staircases. The main one, a heavy spiral near the
music room at the front of the house, had been used by
family and friends. Just inside the butler's pantry, however, a second, narrower one had been used by servants.

Leading the way up, Aunt Suke stopped on the
landing between the third and fourth floors and pressed
on one of the panels in the wall. A door popped open,
and she pulled it wide, revealing a small room no more
than five feet wide and ten feet deep. They both had to
duck to get through the door, so April guessed the
ceiling to be just under six feet high.

The room smelled of cedar and old cloth. Shelves
lined the back wall, and Aunt Suke pulled a string in
the middle of the room, turning on a small yellow bulb
in the ceiling. Returning to the door, she pulled it shut,
latching it on the inside.

"Wow," April whispered. "This is great."

Aunt Suke braced her back against one wall, then slid to a seated position. "Have a seat. We'll stay here until either Polly or the cops give the all clear."

"What is this? Part of the Underground Railroad?"

Aunt Suke shrugged. "Possibly but unlikely, even though one of the western routes flowed close to here. I haven't found anything in the family papers that would indicate it, and besides, the house was built before the Railroad was active in this area, and this is part of the original building."

"So just for storage?"

"More likely for hiding valuables. Caralinda was on the western frontier for a long time, and there were a lot of raiders. I'd think more likely it was storage for the valuables or hiding in case of a raid. There are three of these rooms in the house. They're between the floors." Aunt Suke pointed toward the back of the room. "The only reason my sister and I thought it might be a part of the Underground Railroad is that sometime in the 1850s, a panel was cut back there and a ladder added that leads down to the coal room in the basement."

"That's why you told Daniel there are plenty of hiding places."

Aunt Suke nodded. "That guy with the shotgun could look for a year and never find this."

April fingered a rough spot in the wooden floor. "A year." She shook her head. "I just keep thinking…I've done the same thing every morning Levon was in the field the last year. Even this past winter, if he was out there working. I took him coffee when it was cold, lemonade when it was…" A sudden wave of grief washed over her, and tears slid down her cheeks. "He was so good to me. Better than my own father ever was."

"How so?"

April shrugged. Talking about her past had never been one of her favorite topics. "Levon encouraged me to follow my dreams. Told me I could succeed at my business. He talked about his family a lot, and I got the feeling he adored his wife." April shifted uncomfortably. "I never got the impression from anything he said, or anything I heard about him, that he had ever hit her or Daniel. He seemed to have only his family and this town as his focus."

Aunt Suke braced the bat between her feet. "Levon Rivers was the heart of this town. You have no idea how this is going to change Caralinda. This is going to hurt, more than you know."

April raised her head, eyes still burning. "But won't that make it easier to find out who killed him? Surely everyone will want to find his killer. It's got to be local, right? Not only because he knew where Levon would be but that he knows how the police work, that all of them will answer that call? That's what you meant about diversionary, wasn't it?"

The older woman paused. "Yes. He's got to be local. He knew this would leave us open."

The underlying thought hit April, and every muscle in her body tightened painfully. "He's still watching me!"

Aunt Suke rolled one shoulder and stretched her left arm. "Most likely, yes. And probably will until he realizes you're secure. Ray and Daniel will probably figure that out as soon as the shots stop at your house and will be back over here shortly."

"You have a lot of faith in them."

"Ray Taylor is the smartest sheriff Bell County has ever elected. He's still a young snapper, but he was a Marine, then a beat cop and a detective in Memphis. You know about Daniel, right?"

April shrugged. "I know he worked with the Nashville PD for a while."

"Did you know he did two tours in Iraq?"

April shook her head. "I didn't even know he'd been in the military."

"Ask him about it sometime."

"You don't think he'd mind?"

"I think he'll jump at the chance to tell you." Aunt Suke pushed a strand of snowy-white hair out of her face. "April, you're going to discover that Daniel Rivers isn't like most men. In any form or fashion."

"And you think he can protect me?"

"I think he'd take a bullet for you. And not just because it's his job."

April stared at her, about to ask more, when a thudding sound echoed through the walls, followed by one sharp bark. She froze as Aunt Suke picked up the bat and edged toward the door, holding up a finger for silence.

Without warning, they heard a shotgun blast, then riotous barking shattered the brief silence.

Daniel knew he'd made a mistake the minute he saw Ray Taylor's face, even before his cruiser slid to a halt in April's driveway, two other officers pulling in beside him. Ray marched in his direction, stopping him with a hand to his chest as he got out of the car.

"What are y'all doing here? Get back in the car,

Rivers! I don't know who to shoot first—you three or that crazy dispatcher!"

Daniel stood his ground, trying to ignore the fact that all the other officers on the scene were standing out in the open, watching their boss scream at him. "She said you were pinned down! What was I supposed to think?"

Ray dropped his hand, relenting. "Two shots, Rivers." He pointed at a line of trees at the far side of the cornfield. "From over there. Might not have even been him. Could have been some nutso hunter. Or—"

"Or a way to get us all here." Daniel felt suddenly cold.

"So get back on your job, Rivers. You asked for it. Stay with it until you hear from *me* that you're needed elsewhere. You got that?"

Daniel was back in the car before the sheriff could finish the final sentence. As he jerked the cruiser into Reverse and spun it backward, he heard Ray's last shout at him.

"Don't be stupid! Call for backup if you need it!"

I've already been stupid. Grateful that Aunt Suke's house sat just over a rise from the cornfield, he shot up a quick prayer for the women's safety. *Ray's right,* he thought, a tightness constricting his chest. *I'm not thinking straight. Not thinking like a cop. Gotta get this under control.*

He pulled into the driveway, and as he got out, he noticed that the house looked peaceful…but different. Closed off, somehow, and Daniel realized they had closed the drapes. *She's closed down the house.*

Like Ray, Aunt Suke's military background must have made her recognize the danger of all the officers being in one location.

A dog's barks reached him, and Daniel recognized them immediately. Polly. And not a friendly Polly. This was the sound of a K-9 officer in pursuit, the barks moving rapidly away from the house and toward the cornfield. Grabbing the cruiser's radio, Daniel spat out a quick call for backup, then tossed the mike aside as he got out. Pulling his gun, Daniel raced to the rear corner of the house, peering around the edge cautiously.

The back of the house seemed secure. All doors were closed and intact, and the crime scene tape Gage had run across the cellar doors still fluttered in the breeze. He turned toward the cornfield.

Ahead, Polly's white fur flashed like spots of filtered sunlight through the tall stalks. Pointing his pistol toward the sky, Daniel sprinted for the corn, ignoring the slashing leaves as he darted after Polly. He could hear someone crashing through the stalks ahead of the dog.

Daniel fought to follow the sound as best he could, pausing only occasionally to refocus on the direction of Polly's ominous barks before racing forward again. The cornfield felt like a sinister maze, however, with the leaves cutting at his hands, the stalks closing around him and causing even Polly's barks to fade into muffled mush.

Without warning, the barks ended in a sharp yelp, and the field fell silent. Daniel stopped, catching his breath, listening. All remained still for a moment more, then whoever Polly had been chasing went back to pushing aside stalks in an attempt to get out of the field. Daniel waited, honing in on a direction, then resumed the pursuit.

The runner heard him right away and cursed, taking off at a new speed and direction.

West. The road! He must have a truck waiting. Daniel gave up trying to follow the runner and turned west, pushing harder through the stalks. *Get to the road first!* Even if he didn't come out at the same place, that stretch of the paved country road was mostly flat. If he couldn't stop him, at least he might be able to see him, identify him.

Out of breath and sweating hard, Daniel burst out of the cornfield just in time to see an ancient, dark green pickup explode from behind an overgrown magnolia on the opposite side of the road, roaring away from him down the winding country lane. He watched, gasping for breath, as the truck passed Aunt Suke's great mansion and turned away from Caralinda's central crossroads.

Daniel wondered what had happened to his backup, then he remembered that all the officers on the force were behind him, having been called to April's home. His pursuit through the corn had lasted only a few minutes—no time for them to arrive. He caught his breath and pulled a notebook from his pocket, taking down everything he could remember about the truck. He'd never seen it before, and it had no license plate. So it was new to Caralinda.

Straightening and pulling in one more deep breath, Daniel turned back. Time to retrace his steps to find out what had happened to brave Polly.

The way back was easier, since he had cut a rather large swath through the field, crushing stalks left and right. He found where he'd turned toward the road and began a methodical search away from his path, trying to find Polly.

She found him instead, her big white head smeared

with a dash of red. He fell to his knees and grabbed her neck in both hands. "It's good to see you, girl. Sorry you got hurt, but I am grateful you *only* got hurt. Let me see what he did to you."

Polly lowered her head, standing patiently as Daniel ran his fingers through her fur, checking bones and skin. He found only a small cut and a lump on her head. "He must have whacked at you with the gun when you got too close to shoot. Aunt Suke will be able to fix that right up."

She responded with a lick to his cheek and exactly two back-and-forth wags of her thick tail.

"Yeah, me, too. Let's go back to the house."

She didn't nod, but it almost felt as if she did as she took the lead in heading back to the mansion, trotting as if she'd never been touched.

Daniel crossed the wide, green backyard, relishing the coolness that passed over him as he walked beneath the towering oaks and maples. Their thick canopy of leaves shaded most of the yard, the branches even extending over the back porch.

On the porch, April and Aunt Suke waited, a baseball bat clutched tightly in Aunt Suke's left hand. Polly and April passed each other on the steps, Polly taking her place at the older woman's side while Aunt Suke knelt to examine the white shepherd.

April reached for Daniel's arm, her fingers grasping the sleeve. "Are you okay?"

He nodded. "Are y'all?"

"Yes!" Her hand tightened. "We could see it!" She pointed to one of the top-floor dormers. "From up there. We hid at first, but then heard Polly chasing him away from the house, so we came out to see if we could tell who it was."

Hope leaped in him. "You could see him? Who was it?"

She shook her head vigorously. "No, not who he was, but what he was wearing. The cap. It was dark red. And we saw the truck."

Daniel closed his hand over hers. "I've never seen it before, and I can promise you I know every vehicle in this county."

"Not that one," April said softly. "Levon brought it home late yesterday afternoon from somewhere in Kentucky. He said he was going to give it to two of the migrant workers to take home to Mexico. The man who killed your father escaped in Levon's own truck."

SEVEN

Daniel's large hands poised over the keyboard, his broad, strong fingers surprisingly agile as they danced over the computer's keys, confidently moving through the various forms of April's statement. He had already entered in the basic events of the morning and the questions he'd asked Aunt Suke, who'd flatly refused to come to the station until the vet had a look at Polly. He'd double-checked a couple of the details with her, but mostly typed from his own memory...giving April a lot of time to watch the man who'd virtually appointed himself her guardian.

As she watched, the fear and wariness that had gripped April much of the morning began slipping away. She perched on the hard seat of the chair next to the desk Daniel shared with Jeff Gage, occasionally glancing around the cluttered but thoroughly business-like room as Daniel typed. Maybe it was the sense of security she got from being inside the county sheriff's department...or maybe her growing confidence in Daniel gave her a sense of reassurance she'd not felt earlier.

April crossed her arms over her stomach, oddly

aware that her fingers had stopped quivering for the first time since Levon's death.

The sound of clicking computer keys, and the normal buzz of phone calls, rustling paper and the dispatcher's radio calls, however, reminded April that while she might feel safe now, that didn't mean that she'd stay that way. Levon was dead, and his murder had temporarily bonded her to his grieving son while the two of them worked to find the killer before he could come after her again.

April focused on Daniel, noticing the high crisp cheekbones and silkiness of his black hair. Levon had been half-Cherokee, and April could see it clearly in his son. And he was tall, like his father, at least six foot or more. Tall, dark and handsome. Yes, definitely handsome, though she'd never really let herself dwell on that before now.

Strange how you can know someone but never be around him. She and Daniel had met each other a year ago, but she'd deliberately kept her distance, uncomfortable with men around her age—especially attractive men—after her disastrous divorce. She had been unwilling to trust any man at first, even Levon. Letting him into her heart as a neighbor and friend had taken a long time.

April shifted in her chair. The fact that her ex had made her distrust all men gave her yet another reason to despise the man she'd been married to for five years. That and his lying, his affairs and his controlling violence. *A trifecta of reasons,* she thought wryly. No wonder she'd rejected any idea of a date when she'd arrived in town. Daniel had seemed like a good man, but how could she be sure? Once upon a time she'd thought her ex was a good man, too. And thanks to her efforts, her life and Daniel's had seldom crossed, except at the occasional church event or barbecue at Levon's. Like most folks in Caralinda, they both attended the Gospel Immanuel Chapel in the larger community of White Hills, about eight miles down Oak Springs Road.

April cherished her membership at Gospel Immanuel, but she sometimes wished she knew more of the members better. Like Daniel. It was sad to think that she barely knew him, in spite of the fact that he was one of the first people she'd met in town, on the day when he'd helped her move in…

…and asked me out.

April's brows tightened, shading her eyes. Daniel had been interested in her, but she'd held him at bay, still raw from a divorce so difficult it had almost destroyed her faith as well as her finances. Her healing had been slow, and more dependent on her move to Caralinda than she'd wanted to admit at first.

Her need to heal had made her so self-absorbed that it took almost the entire year for her to realize how much Caralinda had to do with that healing—belonging to a good church, having Levon as a supportive neighbor, enjoying the quiet comfort of the country life as she worked to build her business. Some of the solitude had been good for her, as the introspection had allowed her to grow stronger in her faith and closer to God.

But I also isolated myself. Sitting there, April realized she'd never truly become a part of Caralinda as a community. She was acquainted with most of the people living around the crossroads, and her mind rapidly ticked through almost thirty people she said hello to at the grocery store or bank. But she didn't *know* anyone except Levon. She'd even shut her sister June out of her life for several months. With Daniel, she had never asked him about his life, his likes. This morning Aunt Suke had given her more details about him than she'd gotten to hear all year. She didn't know if he liked movies or camping, even what kind of—

"What kind of music do you like?"

Daniel's hands froze over the keyboard, his fingers hanging in midair, like a cartoon coyote who's just realized he's run off the edge of a cliff. He continued staring at the screen, his eyebrows arched in surprise.

April clamped a hand over her mouth, a tiny "oop!" bursting through her fingers as she realized how out of the blue that question must have sounded. Daniel, in fact, had not been part of her convoluted internal conversation about life and death in Caralinda.

Heat shot through April's face, and she slowly dropped her hand away from her mouth. "I guess that seemed to come out of nowhere."

The corner of Daniel's mouth jerked, as if he were fighting back a grin...*or maybe a grimace,* she thought glumly.

"I did sort of wonder how you got from the description of a green truck to my musical tastes."

April twisted her hands together in her lap. "Aunt Suke warned me that this would happen. She said that I'd want to think about anything other than what happened in the field, so my mind would wander. She was right. Now it's going ninety miles an hour. I can't seem to stop it bouncing from one thing to another."

Daniel finally raised his head to look at her, his brows crunched in concern. "Are you okay? Do you need anything?"

Just as it had that morning when he'd arrived at Aunt Suke's house, the mix of sorrow and compassion on Daniel's face triggered a wave of grief for April. Tears flooded her eyes and overflowed as she gasped out just one word.

"Levon."

Daniel's face blanched, but he reacted as if an alarm had sounded. He burst from his chair and pulled April to her feet. Wrapping one arm protectively around her, he guided her into one of the interrogation rooms and shut the door. Then he folded her into his arms, pressing her firmly against his chest. April, grateful for the sudden reassurance, the engulfing *safety* of the hug, clutched his shirt as great sobs racked her, tears flooding from her eyes and clogging her nose, wondering why she only seemed to feel comfortable enough to cry when she was in his arms.

Daniel stroked her hair, tightening his hold on her. "I know, sweetheart. I know. It's okay." As her sobs began to ease, he spoke again, her hair muffling his soft voice. "You've been so strong, first in the fields, and then with the attacks on your house and Suke's. It's okay to let it go now. You're safe here."

She sniffed, then raised her face, pushing back from him a bit. "What about you? He was your father."

Daniel brushed tears from beneath her eyes with one finger, then pulled a handkerchief from his pocket and handed it to her. "I lost it at the scene. Ray gave me the time. It helped me pull it together."

She clutched the handkerchief as if it were a life vest. "At least you only fell apart once."

Daniel shook his head. "It'll probably happen again, for both of us. Grief tends to come in waves, hitting you unexpectedly just when you think you're doing all right. I was expecting this—once you got past the adrenaline overload from the shooter's other attacks, it's natural that you'd go back to remembering what you've lost."

April wiped her eyes. "He meant the world to me. As much as my own father." She paused and sniffed. "More."

Brushing a strand of damp hair from her face, Daniel eased back a bit. "Then let's find out who killed him."

She shook her head. "I really don't remember."

"But you will." Before she could protest, he pressed on. "*You will.* Just like with the green truck. You saw it…you remembered something about it."

April wondered if she looked as skeptical as she felt. "I don't think—"

"I want to try something, if you're up to it. Just like the truck led to a tidbit that could be useful, when you see other things associated with my dad, you may remember more details."

April felt confused by his words and a little dizzy again. "I'm not sure I understand."

With growing enthusiasm, Daniel pulled her to the table in the room and pulled out a chair. As she sank into it, he pulled the other one around to the same side and sat facing her. "Look, I think everyone agrees this has to be local. It wasn't a stranger who just wandered into that field to shoot my dad. Right?"

April nodded, and Daniel continued. "He knew when my dad worked that field and which days he'd be alone, without the migrant workers helping him. My dad knew him. He had to. He never would have let a stranger carrying a shotgun get that close. But you're still a newcomer here. You haven't lived with these folks all your life, to the point where you'd recognize someone just by the shirt he wore. All these farm boys with their jeans and ball caps all look alike from the back, especially when you're just getting to know them. But I think you've at least met him, and the right context will trigger the right memory."

He had a point, and April leaned back in the chair to contemplate it. He was right about the truck, as well. If she had not seen the truck, she wouldn't have even thought about it, much less tied it to Levon's murder. Maybe there were things lurking in her head....

"What did you have in mind?"

"Where all did you go that Dad was there, as well? Especially recently."

April frowned, thinking over the past few months. "Why recently?"

"Because I don't think this is about something that happened a long time ago. Just a gut hunch."

April nodded. "I can see that." She took a deep breath and counted off places with her fingers. "Church. Mostly Wednesday nights and Sundays, but there was that big blowout barbecue to welcome the new senior pastor a few months ago. Then I went with him a couple of Saturdays to the park, to watch baseball. If I remember, we were there because your cousin was playing—"

"Bobby. He played for a farm team after college, then he threw out his shoulder."

"—and a guy you grew up with. Levon said he was your best friend."

"That would be Kip. He plays shortstop. I think those guys have been playing together since they were... What's wrong?"

April's gaze had wandered from Daniel's face to a spot on the wall behind his head, while her mind had drifted back several weeks. A feeling of dread washed over her and her fingers quivered. "The team. They all wore red hats. You don't think it could be one of—"

Daniel grabbed her hands suddenly, and April started back to the present. "Listen to me closely." He put his face directly in her line of sight, his black eyes focused solely on hers. He cupped her face with one hand so that she couldn't turn away. "We already suspect the killer is local. Someone we know. I don't want you to ignore any insight you may have, any memory. You can't let them throw you, no matter what they tell you. Memories can't hurt you, and I'm going to make sure the present doesn't, either. I'll protect you."

The soothing warmth of his palm had its intended effect, and April took a deep breath, willing herself to stay calm. "Okay. I don't really mean to wig out every time I remember something. And I know that every guy in town may have a red hat in his closet."

He nodded. "At least two ball teams, two corporations…and anyone who's a fan of the University of Alabama."

"I thought this was mostly University of Tennessee country. Big Orange."

Daniel sat back and rested one arm on the table. "Mostly. I'm sure quite a few make the trek to Leyland Stadium every fall Saturday, but there are a lot of Tide folks around. The point being—"

"Lots of red hats."

"Lots of red hats," he repeated. "Important, but I'm convinced you'll recognize other things, as well. Something about his stance or his walk." His eyes narrowed as if he'd just thought of something. "Did he say anything?"

"Not really. Just the threat in the basement."

"Do you think you'd know his voice?"

April let her thoughts go back. She shook her head. "Even when he threatened me in the basement, it sounded nothing like a normal speaking voice."

Daniel examined her face a moment, then nodded, as if convinced there was nothing more to pursue in that line of questions. He stood and offered April his arm.

She got to her feet as well and slipped her hand into his elbow. "Now what?"

"Now we start our Levon-inspired tour of Caralinda, with maybe a side trip or two. Keeping you safe, of course."

April let herself smile. "Of course."

He led her out of the interrogation room and through the bull pen, ignoring the looks from the officers and Martha as he opened the front door. As they started toward his cruiser, he cleared his throat. "Sixties and seventies classic rock. Some folk. A little country, a little Southern gospel."

A lilting laugh burst from April, and she squeezed his arm tightly. "Me, too, for the most part. I like a bit of classical, too, and some of the new indie Christian rock bands. Do you like Creedence, like your dad did?"

"My dad was in Vietnam, did he tell you? That's where he learned to like CCR."

She nodded. "One day I was helping him clean up after one of those two-day barbecues and I found a box of pictures. I bribed him with a Coca-Cola cake with caramel icing, and he started telling tales."

"Ouch. You knew his soft spot."

April shrugged. "It was, for a bit. Then his girlfriend started making them on a regular basis and I had to switch to blueberry muffins. Carla can't make muffins at all. Burns them every time."

Daniel froze in his tracks so suddenly that April's hand jerked from his arm as she kept walking.

She turned to face him. "What's wrong?"

He swallowed hard. "He had a girlfriend?"

April's eyes widened. "You didn't know? She was at the last barbecue. Carla. Carla Godsey. She was in his Sunday-school class at church." The stunned look on his face confused her. "You really didn't know?"

Finally he shook his head. "No. Or that would have been our first stop."

"Why?"

"Carla Godsey has three sons and a daughter."

She nodded. "I know. Met them at church. Nice kids."

"Did you know her youngest son plays football for the University of Alabama?"

April didn't, but she remembered all too well meeting the three young people at the last barbecue. She shook her head. "No. That one I wouldn't believe. Those three acted as if Carla going out with your dad was one of the best things that had ever happened to her." She shook her head again. "No."

He acknowledged her certainty with a quick nod of his head, but he picked up his pace toward the cruiser. "Still, Ray should talk to them. I'll radio him and let him know that—" His voice broke off when a sound that April had already heard too much of that morning shattered the air around them.

Gunfire.

The windshield of Daniel's cruiser splintered, and he grabbed April, throwing her to the ground, calling for help. Screams of other people on the street echoed off the buildings as they ran for cover. A second shot fractured the front glass of the sheriff's department, and officers flooded from the building, guns drawn, taking cover behind the cars, eyes scanning the buildings and cars up and down the street.

April pressed her cheek against the hot sidewalk as tears flooded her eyes. *Please, God,* she prayed feverishly. *I can't live like this. I can't live in fear. I can't.*

EIGHT

Daniel watched Jeff Gage question a business owner across the street. Only the two shots had been fired, and once they were convinced the attack was over, deputies had searched through storage rooms, on roofs and in empty lots trying to find the gunman's location. Other officers had canvassed the shop owners on the small square, but none of them had seen anyone suspicious. No one carrying a gun. He'd finished giving his own statement to Ray that, no, he hadn't seen anyone on the street or any of the buildings. Until they'd emerged from the station, they had been in an interrogation room, away from all outside windows.

Daniel looked around at April, who sat on the sidewalk, her back pressed against the hot brick of the building and her knees drawn tight to her chest. With strands of silky hair dangling around her face, she looked very much like a lost little girl.

Ray returned to his side, looking down at April. "She needs to go inside."

"I tried. She refuses."

With a long exhale of frustration, Ray walked over to April. "Ms. Presley, you need to go inside the station.

We have to take this threat seriously. You could have been killed."

April looked up at him, the stress showing in the tight skin around her eyes, the way color had washed from her face, except for twin blotches of red high on her cheekbones. But her voice remained calm. "You want me to hide again? Cower somewhere in fear, knowing he'll come after me again the minute I'm in range? All I've done all day is hide. I can't do it anymore. We're not supposed to live in fear."

"So what do you want to do?" Daniel asked, squatting down beside her.

She turned to face him. "I want to go on that tour. I want to figure out who's responsible for this. I want to catch the killer, and see him convicted and know that it's safe again to live my life and mourn my friend without having to worry about a gunman hiding in every shadowy corner."

"Tour of Caralinda?" Ray shook his head. "No. It isn't safe to have you wandering around town."

April frowned. "I believe that between God and your officers, I'll be okay. Don't you?"

Ray froze, his eyes hard, and for a full thirty seconds, only the muscle in his jaw jerked.

Daniel managed to keep a straight face by biting the inside of his lower lip. *Talk about an unanswerable question!*

Ray did an almost military-precise about-face and returned to Daniel. "She's almost as stubborn as her sister."

Daniel's eyebrows arched in curiosity. Maybe the rumors about the sheriff and April's widowed sister June were true, but Daniel also knew the danger of asking Ray questions about his private life. The day was tense enough already.

"I want to take her to the baseball field in Caralinda, then to Aunt Suke's."

Ray cut his eyes toward April, then back to Daniel. "Explain."

Daniel summed up his plan to Ray, ending with why he'd agreed to let her stay at Lucretia Stockard's home. After a moment, Ray nodded. "We certainly don't have the manpower to stage a full safe-house situation. Not while still addressing the threat and investigating the murder. Suke's right about that much. Her place is probably safest in lieu of one." Ray crossed his arms. "But your plan to stimulate her memory is high-risk. Especially now. You'd basically be dangling her as bait."

Daniel motioned toward his cruiser and the two that sat beside it. "This guy is local. He knew where we were, set up a sniper position, got away afterward and no one noticed him. You know everyone on the square would have noticed a stranger. Everyone knows everyone in Bell County. It's the way it's always been."

Ray hesitated, then looked at April again. "And with that stubborn streak, she's not going to stay cooped up for long, no matter where we put her. You turn your back and she'll be scooting out Suke's back door and across that field."

Daniel shifted his weight to his left foot. "There's a game this evening. Little League, but a lot of parents will be there. I know where I can park so she doesn't have to be out in the open. I hope something else will jog her memory…the way someone walks…or something. You never know what could trigger a memory."

He filled Ray in on what April had remembered so far, including the red hat and the green truck.

Ray's expression sharpened. "Did she know who Levon planned to give the truck to?"

"Brothers. Julio and Antony Reyes. Both are in the country legally, but they still have family in Mexico."

"Could they be suspects?"

Daniel thought a moment about the two brothers who'd worked so hard with his dad over the past few years. Finally he shook his head. "I don't think so, but you should talk to them. See what they know. They're good men—migrant workers who come here every year. Julio is virtually Dad's foreman, in charge of the other workers. He has a kid in Mexico with a heart problem. They can't afford the medical help they need with jobs there, which is why they come over here. Dad's helped them with steady work, and I guess that's why he'd want to give them a truck. I can't see them having anything to gain from hurting him."

"But they may know something. Or they may have a motive we don't know about. We still don't have a clue about the *why* of this."

Daniel nodded. "They usually know everything that's going on. Definitely worth asking." Daniel also filled Ray in on Carla Godsey, information the sheriff absorbed silently. "You might want to talk to her youngest son."

Daniel paused. "Do you mind if I talk to Kip and Bobby about this?"

Ray's face looked like a frown engraved in stone. "Why?"

"Just a hunch. They both worked with Dad this spring, during the planting. They might remember if he had someone new working, someone who might know why he decided to plow under half his field."

Ray stared at his deputy a moment, then nodded once. "Just to find out if they might have leads. Do *not* follow up on anything. Bring me the info."

"You got it."

Ray turned to April again, then pulled a set of keys out of his pocket and handed them to Daniel. "Take my truck to the game. You obviously can't drive the cruiser, and my truck might be less obvious than anything you or April own. When we're done, I'll check on the Reyes brothers." He looked Daniel up and down once. "Change clothes before you go to the park. With you in uniform you might as well put a target on her back. And put her in a vest before you take her anywhere."

April agreed with Ray's wishes, accepting a loan of a bulletproof vest from one of the female deputies before leaving the station. By the time they'd arrived at Daniel's house, April felt as if she had covered every inch of Bell County, and the day wasn't over yet. Levon's murder, which had happened not far from the heart of Caralinda, already felt very far away in time as well as distance, given all that had happened since then.

Daniel's home lay close to the county's eastern edge near White Hills, about a twenty-minute drive from Bell Springs, where the sheriff's office was located on the western side of the county.

An ache gripped April just below her heart, and she bit her lower lip as she gazed out the truck's window, watching as corn and soy bean fields, as well as acres of tobacco, slid by.

Levon had loved the land with a passion, loved planting and watching crops grow. Just last week, he'd talked about his current crop with the enthusiasm of a small boy with a new game. He'd also idly wished Daniel would come back to the farm.

"Why did you give up farming?"

Daniel glanced sideways at her only once, then returned his focus to the road. "That was my father's dream. Not mine."

April twisted in her seat to look more directly at him. "What was your dream?" When Daniel hesitated, she asked quietly, "Music?"

His mouth tightened. "What makes you think that? Just because we're close to Nashville doesn't mean everyone wants to be in the music business." He straightened a bit as he swung the truck through one of the extreme turns inevitably created when field roads are paved and turned into streets.

Her brows crunched together at the hostile tone. "I know it's a cliché, but I grew up in East Nashville, remember? I know the town doesn't really revolve around the industry, and that a lot of people play who aren't in it professionally." She sat straighter, bothered by her own defensiveness. "But you sing in the choir, with a beautiful voice. And your left fingertips are callused. That said 'strings' to me. Guitar? Mandolin?"

The muscles in Daniel's face softened. "Sorry. Years of people asking me about it has had an effect." He paused, then sighed. "I thought about it. Everyone told me I had the talent."

"You do. I love your voice. Every time you do a solo, it makes the hair stand up on my neck, like I'm moving a little closer to God."

Daniel hesitated, his cheeks reddening slightly. "Thank you."

"So why didn't you pursue it?"

He shrugged one shoulder. "I just always wanted to be a cop. Never felt a pull to be anything else, even as a kid. The music was a gift from God, but I never felt called to take it outside the church. As for farming, it was just something to do until I could get out of here. So when I graduated from high school, I headed for the criminal justice department at Middle Tennessee State."

April turned again to look at him more directly, truly intrigued by his story. She found herself watching each contour, every line of his face for changes in his expression. "Then?"

Daniel fell silent a moment, glancing at her only once. "Then 9/11 happened."

"Oh." April felt her chest tighten, and her voice softened. "Aunt Suke said you'd done two tours in Iraq."

Daniel nodded, then aimed the truck down a thin country road, barely wide enough for two cars. "I enlisted that September. When I came back, I joined the Nashville police department for a couple of years, then moved back up here."

"Why did you move? After Iraq and Nashville, this has to be a lot different."

This time Daniel's silence went on for some time. Another turn, then Daniel steered the truck into the driveway of a small, tidy ranch home. The simple but pristine landscaping made it looked well tended without being overdone. No flowers or frills, just a variety of strategically placed shrubs and monkey grass. A man's house.

Daniel cut the engine, but sat in silence a moment, staring at the house. After a moment, he cleared his throat. "For most of my life, I wanted to get away from here. Do something bigger. Like most kids, I guess."

He turned to look at her. "After Iraq and Nashville, I finally realized that it wasn't Caralinda I wanted to get away from. It was me that I was not satisfied with. Through the experiences I had away from here, I grew up. God let me stumble through enough to open my eyes. I saw that I could do more here where I knew the people and the land than I could in a strange city. That doing something bigger than myself had nothing to do with cities or mission trips or any of that. It had to do with focusing outside me and on the folks God leads me to help. It's trusting, not running away."

April, who had run from the city and a bitter divorce, felt her breath catch in her throat. She stared at him, lost for words.

Daniel leaned back, his cheeks tinged with pink. "Sorry. I didn't—" He stumbled over the words, and one hand gripped the steering wheel tightly. "I didn't mean to get on my soapbox. I do that sometimes." He looked away from her out at the house. "Just ask the guys at the station. They've all heard it."

April searched, and found the quiet words she wanted. "I like your passion. When I hear passion like that, I know it's a God thing."

Daniel looked down a moment, as if he couldn't face her, then, with a sudden movement, he released his seat belt and opened the door. "Hang tight and I'll help you down."

He got out and April waited until he came around and

opened the door. She took his hand and he grabbed her elbow as she slid down out of the truck. "Thanks. The last time I got out of a truck this tall, I sprained my ankle."

Daniel snorted in amusement as he shut the door. "Believe me, we've all given Ray a hard time about buying this tank."

April glanced back at the full-size pickup with the extended cab. It looked as fierce as Ray did himself. Coated with an unusual flat black paint, the truck had the dark tinted windows euphemistically called "privacy glass," making it impossible to tell who was inside. Four spotlights graced the top, with another one mounted to the driver's mirror. Ray had installed roll bars on the bed and added a black steel grill that looked as if it could ram through a concrete wall. "Did he mention his reasoning for buying this?"

Daniel pulled his house keys from his pocket. "Yeah, he said he planned to scare the Thanksgiving stuffing out of a few of our local drug dealers. The windows are bullet-resistant. The engine is modified to be quieter than usual, but it has an off-road suspension."

"Good for sneaking up on folks."

"Something like that."

"And he didn't insist you take it just because your cruiser has a smashed windshield?"

"More like he's as determined to keep you safe as I am."

They entered the house from the carport on the north end, through a door leading directly into the kitchen. Daniel pulled a chair from under a 1950s-style table. "Would you like something to drink while you wait? Water? Soda?"

April craved more than water at that moment, and

the stress and weariness of the day's events let her abandon her manners. "Actually, I'm starved."

Daniel's eyes widened in surprise, and his gaze darted to the clock on the stove: 4:23. "I'm sorry. In all the chaos, I forgot about lunch."

"We both did. All I've had since breakfast was a couple of Aunt Suke's cookies. I was hoping that, maybe, you know, on the way to the ball field, we could stop—"

"How do you feel about grilled cheese sandwiches?"

April brightened. "I love a good grilled cheese. Do you know where we can get one?"

He nodded, as if suddenly deciding on a course of action. "You wait here."

With that, he disappeared down a hallway, and April sank down in the chair, every muscle revealing exactly how exhausted and hungry she was. If it weren't for the stress tightening every sense, she could have easily taken a nap. Instead she took a deep breath, trying to find her second wind, and looked around Daniel's home.

Clearly the house had never seen a woman's touch. The kitchen was Spartan and practical, holding only the bare necessities of modern life.

The spotless nature of the surfaces surprised her—most single men she knew didn't seem to know how to wipe down a countertop. But then again, Levon had always kept his place tidy. He'd said that he'd gotten in the habit when his wife was sick, since watching him learn to cook and clean had always made her smile. Daniel had, apparently, taken to the lessons as well—at least, as far as cleaning went.

Wonder how much cooking he really does. Then, her

natural curiosity—and her innate nosiness—drove her to open the fridge and take a peek.

"Wow." She let out a low whistle.

The stuffed shelves of the refrigerator teemed with fruits, vegetables and containers of meat, milk and condiments. Bottles of marinades, pickles and jellies clustered in the door shelves.

"The cheese is in the top crisper."

April yelped and whirled, gaping up at a grinning Daniel. He'd changed into jeans and a beige cotton work shirt, which he finished buttoning as he looked down at her.

"Uh—"

"You want to help, right? That's why you're looking in the fridge?"

Blankly she nodded. She grasped for another reason, one that might make her look a little less nosy, but she didn't want to lie. "I'm happy to help." She hesitated, his words about the cheese sinking in. "You're going to cook?"

With April still standing in front, he reached over the top of the door and pulled a can from one of the shelves. He opened it and handed it to her as she stepped away from the fridge. "Sure. Quicker and cheaper than a restaurant."

He turned back and started pulling out cheese and butter from the shelves. "By the way, when I was changing, I realized that you might want to clean up some, too. Rude of me not to let you go first."

"You weren't being—"

"Bobby left a shirt here the last time he stayed over. He's a lot smaller than I am, so I thought it might fit better than one of mine. It'll still be big on you and fit a little funny, but it'll probably still look better on you than on my cousin."

"Thanks."

Daniel's cheeks reddened slightly, and they fell silent, staring at each other a moment. April felt abruptly caught by the affection in his dark eyes. She didn't know how to handle it. Some of the other single men in Caralinda had made their interest in her clear, but their looks had never made her feel like this. She tried to rationalize the odd feeling away.

We're clinging to whatever's normal. We keep running to whatever grounds us. There's nothing strange about us finding that comfort in each other...is there?

April asked softly, "Where is it?"

Daniel's soft expression remain fixed on her. "What?"

"The shirt."

He jerked, eyes focusing. "Oh! Yeah. Um, it's on the towel rack in the bathroom." He pointed down the hall. "Second door on the left. I'll get the sandwiches started."

April broke the connection between them, putting her soda on the table and turning to follow his directions to the bathroom. Like the rest of the house, it was compact but sufficient, clean and modestly decorated. Yet it was very bare, almost impersonal. Very different from what she'd expected.

What had I expected? Maybe a version of Levon's house. April shook her head as she entered the bathroom. That would make no sense, she realized. Maddie and Levon Rivers had lived in that house for more than thirty years, and Maddie had left her stamp on every wall, every window, every surface. Levon had changed little since her death, and beloved photos graced anything flat enough to hold a frame. Candles, doilies and the amazing number of crèches Maddie collected still dotted each room.

Daniel had never been married and had not been in the house long enough to collect many possessions. The sparse efficiency of it appealed to April.

She closed and locked the door, noticing that Daniel had also left her a clean washcloth and towel alongside a blue cotton shirt on the rack. *You are anything but thoughtless, Daniel Rivers!*

Her own T-shirt smelled like field dirt and sweat, and she dropped it on the floor as she cleaned up and slipped on the vest, then Bobby's shirt, which was, in fact, too big for her. She paused, sniffing the neckline. She recognized the refreshing scent of the same laundry detergent that Levon had used…the one she used. *Wonder if detergent runs in families…*

April shook away the odd thought, ran her hands through her hair and grabbed the filthy shirt off the floor. Returning to the kitchen, she asked, "Do you have a bag I could borrow for the dirty laundry?"

He turned from the stove, where the sandwiches sizzled in a skillet and a pot of something that smelled delicious bubbled temptingly. He pointed at a drawer near the stove. "Used plastic grocery bags. Help yourself. I found some leftover chicken soup in the fridge. Hope you like it."

She nodded and pulled one out, dropping her shirt in and tying it off. "Smells delightful. Thanks for the loan, too. Being in a clean shirt does help, even if it is a little big."

Daniel flipped the sandwiches over, then glanced at

her again. "Yeah, but it definitely looks a lot better on you than Bobby."

She grinned. "Thanks." She motioned at the skillet. "For the food, too. Do you cook a lot?"

Daniel lifted the sandwiches out and placed them on sturdy white plates. He then dipped into the pot with a soup ladle and poured steaming chicken soup into matching white bowls. "Well, I'm single, and I hate eating out. I despise fast food, and the restaurants around here are okay, but they get old in a hurry. That left two choices—learning to cook or starving."

"Not a big fan of starving?"

"Not my preference, no. And I discovered that cooking is a lot like chemistry, which I was good at in high school."

"Is that when you tried to blow up the lab by throwing a chunk of potassium into a sink of water?"

"Ha! Dad told you about that?"

"One of his proudest moments, I can tell you."

"Yeah, he was so proud he grounded me for three months, and I had to pay for the damages by working nights at a convenience store." Daniel brought the food to the table. "Would you grab another soda?"

"Just don't blow it up." As Daniel laughed, April opened the fridge for another. "Have to admit I'm not used to anyone around here using 'soda' to describe our favorite carbonated delights."

He took it from her and popped the top. "That's my mom's doing. Her family was from Michigan and they all refused to let me call every drink by the same name."

"Is that the same reason you didn't call your father 'Daddy,' like every other good ole boy around here?"

Daniel grinned and pulled out a chair from the table,

motioning for her to sit. "Absolutely. I still remember Mom telling me I was too old for that. I was nine or ten, somewhere in there. Came as a complete shock."

April sat and tugged the chair closer to the table. "How did your *daddy* feel about the change?"

Daniel shrugged one shoulder as he sat down, then closed his fingers lightly around his soda, turning the can a bit. "He didn't interfere too much with instructions she gave me. He appreciated her wisdom."

"Which made him a wise man."

Daniel looked at her, tilting his head to the left, curiosity in his eyes. "You say that like it's an unusual trait."

April chewed her lower lip a second, staring at the crispy sandwich in front of her. "In my experience, it is."

"Your dad wasn't wise?"

She toyed with her silverware a second, then pushed it away from her fidgeting hands. "My father was… smart."

"Intelligence doesn't always equal wisdom."

April looked at him, derision shading every word. "You've got that right."

Daniel reached over and took her hand. "What happened?"

April hesitated, not wanting to relive, or even remember, any of it. *But maybe it's time for him to know why I turned him down.* She took a deep breath and plunged on.

"My father had some serious control issues. And he was violent. He drove my mother into an early grave and my sister June into a rebellion that lasted until Jackie Rhea Eaton pulled her out of the gutter. He drove away every boyfriend I had until I met my husband, and Father only approved of him because my husband was one of his employees. Our youngest sister, Lindsey, fared better because she saw what happened to us."

She paused for a breath. "I should have known what to expect when Father approved of my marriage, but I didn't. My ex had a lot in common with my father. In five years he had three affairs, and I had a broken arm and a dislocated shoulder. I had to get out of the marriage. I had to get out of Nashville."

Daniel stared at her, his eyes wide and his mouth a thin line. His hand tightened on hers. "Where is he now?"

"Oregon. The divorce angered my father to the point where he turned on my ex, who took a new job in Portland. He can't hurt me anymore."

Daniel tapped his plate with his knife, and his words emerged through clenched teeth. "Him hurting you wasn't exactly what I had in mind."

As his meaning sank in, April felt a warm rush of comfort. She returned the squeeze of his hand. "He wouldn't be worth it. But thank you."

"You deserve better."

"That's what Levon tells me."

"I bet you and Dad talk a lot."

"I love talking to him." April grimaced as she noticed their slip into the present tense, then chewed her lower lip and looked down at her plate.

After a moment Daniel cleared his throat, breaking the awkwardness. "Do you want to say grace, or should I?"

April hesitated, not really wanting to explain that no one in her life but Levon ever said grace anymore. She only prayed silently these days. Did she really want to admit how out of practice she was at saying even the simplest prayer out loud?

"It's okay," he said softly. "I know you're worn-out." With that, he bowed his head.

"Lord, thank You for this food and bless it to the nourishment of our bodies. Thank You for keeping us safe so far, and, Lord, I pray You take my father into Your arms and reward him for his love for You. Please sustain us, and help us through this dark time. All this I ask in the name of Your Son, Jesus Christ. Amen."

Daniel squeezed her hand but did not release it. April opened her eyes, even though they stung with tears, and looked at him. Her voice cracked in her throat as she whispered, "That was a great prayer."

He met her gaze. "Dad taught me."

She nodded and held tightly to his hand, which felt firm and gentle under her fingers. "We're going to get through this. One way or another."

"And I'm not going to let him hurt you. I promise. *I promise.*"

"I know."

Then they ate, mostly in a comfortable, comforting silence. As they finished and began cleaning up the kitchen, April finally mustered the nerve to ask Daniel for a favor.

"Do you mind if we take a short side trip before going to the game?"

Curiosity lit his eyes, along with a touch of wariness. "What kind of side trip?"

"Trust me."

NINE

"You want to go to the church." Daniel's voice revealed the curiosity April's request had piqued in him. "Why?"

They stood by the passenger side of the truck, and she peered up at him, a glimmer in her green eyes. "You are the one who wanted to tour the big city of Caralinda in an effort to make me remember something I can't. Right?"

He nodded. "But the idea is that you'd see something or someone who would trigger a memory."

April put a hand on his arm, and Daniel realized that he truly liked looking into those eyes. "Let me try my imagination instead," she said softly. "The church was the last place I had a chat with your dad. Let me see if being there will help me remember more. It's worth the try."

Daniel hesitated, then agreed. *It would be worth at least a try.* "How will we get in?"

"I have a key."

Daniel straightened in surprise. "Why do you have a key to the church?"

April grinned. "I'll explain when I get there."

He opened the door of the truck and helped her in. "This I have to hear."

In the height of summer, night didn't settle on Bell County until almost nine, so a soft, golden light from the west still illuminated the walls and windows of Gospel Immanuel Chapel when they turned into the sloping driveway. The newly paved parking lot, dark and smooth as glass, made for an almost silent ride up to the front door, adding to the feeling of reverence that surrounded the building.

April pointed to an entrance near the office instead of the chapel's front doors. "Park over there." As they got out, April dug into her jeans pocket for her keys, shaking them loose and picking out the one for the church's side door.

"So tell me why you have your own key." Daniel's puzzlement about this particular side trip deepened.

April smiled as she inserted the key and turned it in the lock. Letting the door close behind her, April entered the first room on the right and flipped open the cover of a keypad. She disarmed the alarm system, then flipped the cover shut again.

"Right now, I'm just glad I'm still such a city girl that I don't even leave my house to go to the mailbox without locking the door. Otherwise, my keys would still be in my house with the rest of my stuff."

She led the way down a darkened hall, then took a left.

"You're headed for the choir room."

April looked over her shoulder. "Thought you'd recognize it."

"But I didn't know you would. You don't sing in the choir. You still haven't told me why you have a key."

"Did Levon ever tell you why I was in Caralinda?"

"Just that you were getting over a divorce and needed to get out of Nashville."

April stopped and used another key on her ring to open a door labeled simply Choir. "Yes, but 'out of Nashville' covers a lot of territory. He never mentioned why I chose Caralinda?"

Daniel thought back over all his chats with Levon about her, but nothing came to mind. Finally he shook his head.

"This church," she pronounced, moving to the piano in the room and lifting the cover. She pulled the bench out and sat down. "When June came here as the pastor's wife, I visited a lot. I knew this was a good church, good people. I would have a familiar church to start a new home, and with June's connections, I knew I'd be welcome."

"She's the reason you have a key."

"She knows one of my weaknesses, and when Jackie Rhea died and we got the new pastor, she persuaded the leaders to let me keep it."

With that, April's fingers danced over the keys, releasing a light, delicate sequence of notes that resonated throughout the empty building. She continued playing as she spoke. "She knew I'd miss my piano, which I lost in the divorce, and that even if I could afford a new one—which I can't—I'd never be able to fit one into the cottage."

A complicated arpeggio settled into the steady rhythm of "Precious Memories," a hymn Daniel loved. April sang the melody in a clear alto range that reminded him of some of his favorite gospel singers. Her pitch was perfect, each note and every word carried on an elegant tone. He joined her on the chorus, adding harmony on the thirds of the chords.

They watched each other, almost instinctively falling

into each other's rhythms within the song. As it ended, April closed her eyes, smiling, as if she were absorbing the last tidbits of sound. When she spoke, her words were a bare whisper.

"I love my house, but this is where I come to find peace. To pray. To be closer to God." She opened her eyes. "I'm not always good at showing my faith in public, saying grace or talking about God. But I talk *to* Him all the time. Especially here."

"Dad knew about all this, didn't he?"

April nodded. "He encouraged me, too. In the last few months, he'd even come with me. We'd pray and sing." She paused. "You sound a lot like him."

"Mom used to say that. Why did you lose your piano in the divorce?"

The question caught April off guard, and she stiffened. "I don't think—"

"I really want to know."

April looked down, lips pursed, as she let her fingers caress the keys, almost as if she were touching a beloved child.

"My ex-husband insisted on claiming every musical item in the house in our divorce. The piano, my guitar, every scrap of music. He couldn't even sing in the shower, but he made it a condition of the divorce."

"Why?"

"To punish me." A tear slipped from the corner of her eye. "I caught him cheating, and he hated me for it. When I refused the terms of the divorce that he wanted, he burned everything."

Daniel felt as if she'd slapped him. "He burned it? Are you kidding?"

She shook her head, finally looking up at him.

"Everything. One day while I was at work, he broke in and pulled the piano, the music, the guitar, even my metronome, into the front yard and set them all on fire. The neighbors had to call the fire department to keep the house from going up. He didn't care. It was all about hurting me because I'd caught him sleeping with another woman."

Daniel made a noise deep in the back of his throat that was half growl, half promise of a future injury to her ex. "Was he not charged with anything?"

April shook her head, a grim smile crossing her face. "Setting a fire in a restricted area. He paid the fine and laughed at me in court. We weren't divorced, so there wasn't another legal option. He'd bought the piano and he had the sales receipt to prove it. No law against burning your own stuff."

More tears flowed now, and Daniel sat beside her, pulling April into his arms. "I'm sorry," he whispered.

She remained stiff at first, then slowly melted, her body leaning against his. "Levon encouraged me to join the choir...but I couldn't. I just didn't feel comfortable sharing this part of my life with anyone for a long time."

"So why me?" Daniel felt an odd sense of honor flow through him. "Why now?"

She pushed back and looked at him. Her eyes were still bright but no tears flowed down her cheeks. "Levon always said we'd sing well together. I think he was right."

"So *you* think we blend well?" he whispered.

She nodded. "I think we have a lot we could share."

Daniel could barely breathe. April's beauty had caught his attention a year ago, but her soul, her heart now held him as surely as he held her in his arms.

April reached up and touched his cheek. "But not now. Right?"

Daniel swallowed hard. She was right, of course. Not now. Right now, they were both too raw. Too vulnerable, too fragile with grief. He needed to stay focused, otherwise he wouldn't be able to protect her.

As if reading his mind, April gently pulled away from him and stood up. She closed up the piano, speaking quietly. "Come with me. There's another reason I wanted to come here." Touching his arm lightly, she led the way down the hall toward Gospel Immanuel's Fellowship Life Center. Popping through the double doors, they entered the huge hall, now empty of chairs and tables, their footsteps on the bare tile floor echoing off the concrete walls.

At one end of the room a broad counter opened into a restaurant-size kitchen. Cleaned, empty coffeepots stood guard, waiting for the next church event. April crossed until she was about ten yards from the counter, and she pointed to a spot in front of her.

"Do me a favor and stand here."

Daniel did, watching her closely.

April closed her eyes, her arms limp at her sides. "It was last Sunday. Levon was there, where you are, telling me that he planned to plow under a good portion of the corn. It was dying in the heat. He wanted to try something new—a wheat hybrid."

Daniel, realizing what April needed to do, took a step closer.

"Was anyone around you?"

April hesitated, eyes still closed, tilting her head left, then right, as if mentally peering into the past. "It was coffee time, the crossover period before the last worship service."

"So there were a lot of people around."

She nodded.

Gospel Immanuel held three services on Sunday. Coffee time was between the last two services. This meant that between eleven-thirty and twelve-thirty every Sunday, the Fellowship Life Center overflowed with congregants.

She raised her right arm and pointed toward the counter. "The guys from the ball team were over there. I could hear one of them laughing."

Probably Kip, Daniel thought. The boy always seemed to be laughing about something. "Anyone else?"

"Levon said he spotted Julio and Antony coming in. He was going to talk to them about the truck."

"Do you know if he did?"

She shook her head. "We didn't talk after that."

"Anything else?"

She clenched her eyes, then pointed to the left. "A couple of the guys from the volunteer fire brigade were over there. I remember because June had tried to set me up with one of them a long time ago."

Daniel ignored the twinge of jealousy that shot through him. He'd have to talk to June before too long.

"What about Carla Godsey or her kids?"

April hesitated, then shook her head. "No. They had already left. I think they were having lunch with some relatives down in Franklin."

"Do you remember my father saying anything else?"

April straightened and opened her eyes. "Yes," she said, sounding surprised. "Yes. I just remembered. He was talking about plowing under the corn. He said he wanted Julio and Antony to help, but he didn't think they'd be available since they've been helping a guy up near Clarksville for extra money to send home."

Daniel stiffened. "He said he'd be out in the field alone?"

April nodded. "And that's not all."

Daniel tensed, bracing himself. "What else did he say?"

She stepped closer and laid a hand on his arm. "He said he'd do it today."

Staying at the church hadn't brought on any more revelations, so April and Daniel headed on to the game.

"Didn't know there were this many people in the whole of Bell County," Daniel grumbled as he circled the park a second time.

"Always. I take it you don't get out here much."

"Not if I can help it," he snarled under his breath. "There's no way I'm letting you get out in this crowd."

April pressed her back into the corner where the truck seat met the door, not thrilled about being in the open, either. They had a reason for being here, however. "But what about me being able to see what's going on? See the folks?"

"Leave that to me." As he completed one more circle, he pulled up to a curb behind the concession stand and pushed the truck over the concrete hump. Despite stares and a few annoyed gestures, he managed to ease the truck through the crowd until it pulled up beside the ambulance required to be on duty for all the games.

One of the EMTs started toward them, but another one stopped him, clearly telling the man that it was the sheriff's truck. With a grin and nod, the EMT returned to his station.

"Resourceful fellow," April commented.

"Yep, that's me. Cop, chef and creative about spying on folks."

April grinned at his decision. "In other words, I can see them but they can't see me."

"Not behind this glass," Daniel agreed.

The Caralinda City Park teemed with people. *It does feel like everyone in the county is here,* thought April, amazed that such a small town could bring in so many folks to an evening of baseball and concession-stand food.

Daniel sniffed. "What's that smell?"

April grinned. "Hot dogs and popcorn. Staples of the American diet."

"Glad we ate at the house."

She nudged his arm. "Don't be a snob. There's nothing better than a hot dog at the state fair or a ball game."

"I'll take your word for it."

The park, which covered several acres, featured three full-size baseball diamonds and a soccer field. The three diamonds all backed up against the well-stocked concession stand, putting the food within easy reach of the spectators and their wallets.

April glanced sideways at Daniel and asked, "You really never came out here with Levon? He loved this place."

"I spent time with him on the farm."

"But your friends play."

Daniel shrugged. "And their kids. The guys play on Friday nights, the younger ones on Saturday mornings, the older boys on Saturday afternoons."

"So why don't you come watch them?"

When he didn't answer, she unfastened her seat belt and turned to face him. "Y'know, a man has to have a reason to have a problem with something as simple as baseball."

Daniel stared out at the teams. "Kip and Bobby play on a team sponsored by the Caralinda General Store." He pointed toward a group of red-capped men streaming out of a dugout to take the field.

April glanced at them, then looked back at him. "Subject closed?"

"I think they're called the Drivers. Because of the pizza the store delivers. There's Kip at shortstop. Bobby's at first base."

I guess so. April turned her attention to the field, spotting the guys with the General Store name on their shirts. She loved the Caralinda General Store. It was a catch-all merchandiser left over from the last century, complete with a soda fountain that sold sandwiches, ice-cream treats and pizza. Not long after she'd moved into the cottage, they started offering a delivery service. They even had rooftop signs for their drivers' cars like other pizza places—bright red triangles with the letters *CGS* emblazoned in white, just like the players had on their hats.

"Do any of the team members actually deliver the pizza?"

"Yeah, Bobby makes some extra bucks on the weekends."

"Do you want me focusing on the teams?"

He glanced at her. "Not really, but looking at everyone at once can be overwhelming and distracting. Try looking at groups without really focusing on anyone or anything. I thought it would help to start with

Kip and Bobby's team, since you know some of them. Then the other teams. Then groups like families or clusters of friends."

A twinge of anxiety shot through April. "You know, I still am not sure what I'm looking for."

Daniel turned toward her. "Look at me for a second." She did. "Now, close your eyes. Don't think about anything. Just tell me what's the first thing that occurs to you about me."

April let her lids drop and her mind roam. "Eyes."

"Next."

"Mouth."

"Next."

"Hair."

"What color are my eyes?"

"Black."

"Hair?"

"Black."

"What color is my shirt?"

"Beige."

"What color is the shooter's hair?"

"Blond."

April's eyes snapped open and a hand flew to her mouth as she bolted upright. "I don't believe it!" Her exclaimed words were as breathless as she felt.

"But you still don't remember it, do you?"

April, still reeling from the exercise, thought about that morning's events in the field. Was it really only this morning? She sank back against the seat and shook her head. "No. Do you think I'm right about the blond?"

"I do. And I think you'll start getting flashes like that as time passes. Don't ignore them. Tell me. Write them down. Anything can be a clue."

As she nodded, Daniel scanned the field again. "That's what I want you to do here. Don't so much *focus* on individual people as let them drift across your awareness of a group. How long has it been since you were here?"

April counted back the weeks. "Early spring. I remember because Levon kept talking about what he was going to plant this year."

"So the teams were probably just getting practices up and running."

They fell silent as April let herself recall the spring Friday with the new teams, the freshly mown grass, the squeals of kids and calls of coaches and parents. Her memories moved in and out in bright flashes that were crossed with Levon's murder, the shooter running through the field in front of Polly and Daniel and the roaring green truck.

In the meantime, a world of people in front of the truck circled around the concession stand, dodging dogs, running children, parents with boxes of hot dogs and drinks and, once, a flying ice-cream bar that hit a nearby trash can with a wet splat. Ray's truck was set so high that few of the passersby could have seen into the cab even without the protective glass, and most never even tried. Spectators in the bleachers cheered, and April could hear the metallic *ponk* of a ball connecting with an aluminum bat even through the closed windows of the truck.

Nothing. She tried, letting her gaze wander from this man to that, trying to register the way this man walked or the way that one held his shoulders. She watched men run, stoop, twist and pick up their children. Most of the games had ended, and groups of men stood around, celebrating or criticizing.

After only a few moments, however, every male started to look like another, and a strong sense of dread and confusion began filling her mind. Without warning, tears sprang to April's eyes, and her fingers trembled.

"Daniel, this isn't working."

Concern clouding his features, Daniel reached over, covering her hands with his right one. "What's wrong?"

She shook her head. "I can't do this. I feel…exposed. And I'm failing you."

Daniel squeezed her hands. "No, you're not. What I'm asking isn't easy. I need to talk to Bobby and Kip, but if you can hang on a few more minutes, I'll get you out of here."

April nodded. "Okay."

Pulling out his cell phone, he dialed a quick number, and April watched as, near one of the bleachers, Kip pulled a cell phone from his pocket. In low tones, Daniel asked Kip to bring Bobby and come over to the truck. Kip looked up suddenly, directly at the pickup, then nudged Bobby, indicating that he should follow. Both wore dark red shirts and white baseball pants, their wet hair plastered to their heads. Kip, who was an inch or so taller, and a few pounds heavier, had his dark red cap in one hand, wiping sweat from the back of his neck with it.

"Why talk to them now?"

Daniel looked down at the dashboard for a second, his gaze distant. "I want to find out what they've heard."

"Oh." April closed her eyes a few moments, regret and grief heating her face. What a horrid emotional place she'd found herself in, so immersed in a man's death that she forgot how other people may have reacted, how his loss might have impacted them. Especially in a town this size, where the news of his death must have traveled through the community like a lightning bolt.

She looked up again as the window slid down. The two men outside grabbed the door and stepped up on the truck's running board, their heads and shoulders filling the open window. Kip spoke first.

"Hey, Danny boy. What are you doing in Ray's sweet ride? I thought he'd come to collect Bobby and me for something we didn't remember doing."

Daniel lowered his chin a bit. "You heard about Dad?"

Kip's face crunched into a tight grimace, and for a moment April thought he was about to cry. "Yeah, man. I keep hoping it's not true. Me and Charlie have been calling your house about every hour. Didn't call the cell in case you were on the job with it."

"Yeah. I am. That's why we're here."

Bobby, an inch shorter and a few pounds lighter than Kip, looked at April curiously. "Is that my shirt you're wearing?"

Kip's eyebrows shot up, and he bounced up on his toes as if he were about to leap off the running board. He seemed desperate to talk about anything but Levon. "I do believe it is. Didn't you leave that at Daniel's hou— Hey!"

Daniel grasped Kip's forearm, his fingers digging in. "Stop."

All the hyperactivity seemed to drain from Kip as his gaze locked on his friend's face. "Sorry." He swallowed. "I just keep thinking—"

"He's really gone, Kip. Someone shot him."

Blood seemed to drain from both Bobby and Kip.

Bobby wiped his face roughly, and Kip muttered something dark and harsh under his breath, and his eyes narrowed to slits. "Do you know who?"

"Not yet."

Kip looked from Daniel to April, then back to his friend. He lowered his voice. "So no one saw it?"

"April saw it, but she didn't know who it was. That's why we're here. To see if she recognizes anyone."

Bobby's eyebrows came together over his nose. "You saw Levon get shot?"

April felt a sudden urge to hide, to dig in behind Daniel, but she resisted and straightened her shoulders. *I will not fear this.* "I did, but I don't remember much."

Kip stared at her. "You don't remember? You saw someone shoot a man and you don't remember?"

Daniel held up a hand. "Back off, Kip. Even trained officers can experience a shooting and not remember. It's not uncommon."

"But—"

"No buts. I can't work the case as an investigator, so I'm protecting April, and we're revisiting some of the places she went with Levon. And I want to talk to the two of you. Can you meet us at Aunt Suke's in a couple of hours?"

They nodded. "Sure. We'll do whatever we can. You know all you have to do is ask." Kip hesitated, a look of abrupt dread crossing his face. "Have you told your family yet?"

Daniel shook his head. "No notifications have been made. Just what I know has gone around town."

Kip nodded frantically, then dropped down off the running board. "If you need help, let me know."

"I will. You okay?"

Kip's face scrunched again. "I should get home to Charlie."

"Go."

April watched as Kip ran toward the parking lot, his slowly drying hair beginning to turn golden in the afternoon light.

"Bobby," Daniel said, "would you tell your mom the details? I'm going to call the out-of-town folks tonight."

The younger man nodded. "I'm sorry, Daniel." With that, he turned and left, brushing tears off his cheeks.

"Who's Charlie?"

Daniel cleared his throat and rolled up the window. "Kip's wife. Charlotte. They were both close to my dad." He reached down, released the emergency brake and looked in all the mirrors for wandering Caralindians. "Kip, Charlie and I were like the three musketeers when we were kids. Bobby's a few years younger, but he hung out with us, too, when he was old enough. We went everywhere together, did everything together. Then we turned fourteen, and all of a sudden Kip starting sitting between me and Charlie. They married three years later, still seniors in high school. Two kids and they've been happy as clams ever since."

As Daniel eased the truck out of the park, moving gingerly among the remaining crowd, April looked around, suddenly feeling nervous. Something bothered her about the encounter with Kip and Bobby, something she couldn't quite get her finger on. Besides, being in the park had increased her sense of dread. She had thought they had come to the park to immerse her in memories of Levon, not discuss his death with anyone. She'd felt protected in the big truck until Daniel had lowered the window to talk with Bobby and Kip. Had others on the park grounds been able to see her and Daniel with the window rolled down?

She shook her head, trying to push the feeling away, and she felt a bit reassured by the pressure of the vest beneath the thin T-shirt.

The whole exchange left her feeling uneasy and a touch paranoid.

She straightened in the seat and looked around at the dwindling crowd, trying to remember more about the day she'd been here with Levon. Nothing outstanding came to mind. It'd been a little cool, as early spring is in the rural South. Kip and Bobby had both played that day, but Levon didn't introduce them right away, as he was reluctant to interrupt the game. He talked about them, however, throughout the course of the game. She remembered because he had been so proud of both of them, almost as much as he was Daniel.

Yet both were so very different from the dark-haired son seated beside her. Kip and Bobby were fair, lean, athletic and carefree, whereas Daniel carried a more muscular build that April now realized he must have developed either in police academy or in the military. His calm demeanor left them looking like jokester schoolboys.

Suddenly she got it. April turned to Daniel, knowing she understood. "You left them behind."

Daniel braked the truck, looking at her, then glanced over his shoulder before turning back to her. "What? What did I leave?"

She grabbed his arm. "No. That's why you don't go to the games. Why you won't watch them play."

Daniel sat rigid, staring at her, his face a mask.

April's words picked up speed. "You love them. You

care for them. But they stayed behind. They're just older versions of what they were in high school. You went to college, and Iraq and the police force. They've not seen what you have. It hurts to watch them play because you can't go back to that, to the way you used to be."

Daniel faced forward again, letting the truck roll forward slowly, until he had threaded it from among the people and out onto the highway. He turned on the headlights to push back the deepening night, but the cab of the truck remained quiet as he had turned onto the long country lane leading to Aunt Suke's.

April focused on the tall corn that lined both sides of the lane. Maybe she had gone too far. Maybe she was completely wrong. Either way, she would not speak until he did.

When he finally responded, the firm words held a quiet calm. "My guess is that's a feeling you understand all too well."

Relieved, she nodded. "Maybe we've both met someone who understands what we've been through."

Daniel almost smiled, but his reaction changed to surprised horror as the tall pickup was rammed from behind. "What—"

His words broke off as they were hit again, this time on the right rear fender. "It's the green truck! Get down!"

April curled into a ball, scrunching down below the windows, as the big black truck slid to the left. The green truck hit them again on the right rear fender and kept pushing, skidding the back end of Ray's truck to the left.

The pickup fishtailed, and Daniel fought the wheel hard. But the narrow lane worked against him, and the back tires spun wildly on loose gravel. As he pulled back onto the pavement, the green truck struck again, and the wheel bucked under Daniel's hands. The black truck careened to the other side of the road, burying itself almost up to the axle in the plowed, dry earth of the field.

April felt as if she were a yo-yo as her body bounced with the rocking truck, only to be yanked back by the seat belt. She screeched, and Daniel muttered under his breath as he shoved the gear lever into Reverse and gunned the engine.

Dirt sprayed in tall geysers as the tires spun, digging into the ground for traction. They found it abruptly, and the truck jerked back onto the road, the engine roaring its displeasure. Daniel slung the truck around until they were facing the way they had come, ready to take on his attacker. Instead he twisted in his seat to look behind him, then to either side. He checked the mirrors, still breathing heavily, and April slowly pushed up until she could see out the windows.

The lane was empty, with only the impenetrable darkness around them.

TEN

"What year was the truck?"

"Late sixties. Maybe early seventies."

Ray stood next to Daniel, staring at the damage to the black truck in the distorted purple-white glow of the dusk-to-dawn light illuminating Aunt Suke's front yard.

"Truck frames still had a lot of steel in them back then. He's probably running a rebuilt or new V-8. My guess is he thought he had more weight and enough power to take out the truck and you, then kill April. When he realized you and old Betsy here had too much fight in you, he took off. Retreat for a better time."

"How did he know it was us? Folks around here think you drive it."

"Don't know, Rivers." Ray's voice held a tinge of sarcasm. "How often do you think I call Kip Redding and Bobby Martin over to my truck for a friendly chat?"

Daniel ran his hand through his hair in frustration. "I can't believe I was that dumb."

"Another reason for you not to be involved in this investigation." Ray relented, and his voice lowered. "Daniel, you're a good cop. One of my best. But you're too close to this one. You can't see the big picture."

"They're coming over in a few minutes."

Ray stepped back. "Who?"

"Kip and Bobby. I wanted to get their ideas for who might have had a problem with Dad."

Ray muttered something under his breath and thumped a huge dent in his truck's fender.

Daniel glanced over his shoulder at the house. The long, deep front porch shrouded the house in darkness, but he could still see April's pale face in one window, watching them, her eyes hollow with exhaustion and physical and emotional anguish. He looked back around to see his boss watching him.

"How is she?"

"Pretty frazzled."

Ray's left eyebrow cocked. "Well," he drawled, "let's see. In the past ten hours she saw her best friend shot, had her house destroyed, has been interrogated, shot at and almost killed in a car crash with a maniac. And just when reasonable people might expect, oh, a chance to rest, the man who thinks he's in love with her drags more people into her safe house."

Daniel froze, heat filling his face. "The man who—"

Ray cut him off with a sharp wave of his hand, his frustration boiling over. "Don't, Rivers. Don't even protest. I've watched you get moony-eyed when she's around for months."

"Ray—"

"Look, I'm going to stay around for this little interview session with your friends, and then we're both going home. Tomorrow, I want you to pick her up in the truck and meet me at the station. No later than nine. Are we clear?"

Daniel straightened and almost saluted Ray. "Yes, sir."

* * *

April watched Ray and Daniel talk, recognizing that Ray had taken control of the situation. She wondered if Daniel felt as lousy as she did. She'd blown up at him after the accident, and while she couldn't deny she'd meant what she'd said, she hated to think of the look that had been on his face when she was done.

They had both been silent following the green truck's disappearance. But when they got out at Aunt Suke's, Daniel's rage had burst from him like an explosion, the grief and frustration from the day's events fueling the anger that rocketed out. He'd slammed his hand into the side of the truck, a roar bellowing from deep within.

April, too, gave in to the pressure as she finally realized what had bugged her about the chat with Kip and Bobby. She grabbed Daniel by the arm and spun him around, flattening her hands against his chest and pushing him back against the truck.

"Stop it! Just stop it!" she screamed. Lowering her voice only a bit, she went on, emphasizing her points with short shoves, keeping him pinned against the truck. "We went to the park because you're a cop who's not allowed to be one, because you think I'll remember something I never saw! You're wrong, Daniel. I'll never remember it because I never saw it! Why did you tell Bobby and Kip that I was there? You think they'll keep quiet about it? Now everyone, including the killer, will think I know something I don't!"

Her voice had escalated almost to the point of hysterics. "I don't know who killed your father!"

The devastated look on Daniel's face made April back away, gasping for breath. She sank down next to the truck, hugging her knees to her chest, her face buried against her jeans. Tears flowed, and she refused to look up.

Daniel had called the sheriff about the truck, but they had not spoken to each other since. She watched him, but didn't know if she could speak again, especially not with Kip and Bobby coming to the house.

"You need to come away from the window, girl." Aunt Suke put a gentle hand on April's back. "Even with the lights out, it's not safe."

April nodded, and let the drapes fall shut. She let Aunt Suke guide her to the Queen Anne sofa, where she sank down as if her legs no longer worked. "I'm just so tired. I want to go to bed, but Kip and Bobby are coming over."

"And I'm sure that's exactly what Ray is dressing Daniel down about even as we speak."

April shook her head, her gaze fixed on some far distant place. "He shouldn't."

"Hmm." The older woman sat next to her. "So what did you fight with Daniel about?"

April looked up at her. "How did you know?"

Aunt Suke waved her hand dismissively. "I'm old, but I'm not deaf. I may not have heard every word, but the screaming was hard to miss. What was it about?"

"Aunt Suke, I really don't want to—"

"Nonsense. You don't talk it out, it'll just fester. Have you eaten?"

Wearily April nodded. "Sandwiches at Daniel's."

"Good. Then come with me. We'll indulge in a little instant gratification while we sit in the TV room so you can put your feet up in the recliner. You can tell me about the fight."

"Instant gratification?"

"Chocolate ice cream. You in?"

Even in exhaustion, some things are irresistible. Like recliners and chocolate ice cream. April stood and followed Aunt Suke toward the kitchen.

Kip Redding sat on the Queen Anne sofa in Aunt Suke's parlor, leaning forward and twisting his dark red ball cap between his hands. "Did y'all talk to the Reyes brothers? They worked with him more recently than I did. Since I've been on with the Fleetwood plant, I've not been around much."

Daniel deferred to Ray on that question, fighting a strong sense of irritation that threatened to send him back to his earlier rage, which he still regretted and hadn't had a chance to apologize to April for.

This is a waste of time. What was I thinking? Kip and Bobby had arrived together, somber with grief but ready to talk about Levon. And talk they had. For almost thirty minutes, the two had reminisced about Levon the boss and Levon the friend and Levon the community activist and Levon the farmer.

But nothing about Levon the murder victim. And at that moment he wanted to strangle both of them, a sensation made worse by Kip's and Bobby's casual demeanors and nervous fidgeting. *My father's dead! Help us!*

Ray, who stood near the parlor's arched entrance, nodded. "I spoke with them. Took me fifteen minutes to get them calmed down afterward. What about you, Bobby?"

Bobby twisted on the edge of the matching Queen Anne chair when Ray said his name. "Last time I worked with Levon was over a month ago. We hadn't talked much since, except when he said he probably wouldn't need my help till harvest." Bobby turned to Daniel. "I'm real sorry about Levon, Daniel. If I had known he was going to plow that field under, I would have volunteered to help."

Daniel frowned. "You didn't know he planned to plow?"

Kip straightened up and leaned forward. "I don't think anyone did, Danny. You know we would have all pitched in. No way we would have let him work out there by himself."

"Was it unusual for him to work alone?" Ray asked Daniel.

Daniel glanced at Kip and Bobby, neither of whom offered help on that one.

"Yes," said April from the archway. "It was."

Daniel stood abruptly and went to her side, motioning for her to sit. She looked a bit more collected, but exhaustion still haunted her eyes, and she sat stiffly, crossing her arms over her abdomen.

"How so?" Ray asked.

She swallowed hard. "Of course, he did on occasion do some bits of work alone. Couldn't be helped. But for something like that, for plowing a large section, he almost always had help." She glanced at Daniel, apparently trying to decide whether or not to continue. "He didn't want anyone to worry after last fall."

Daniel stared at her. "What about last fall?"

Kip spit out a nail he'd been chewing. "He fell off a tractor."

Daniel jerked straight, a jolt of shock shooting through him. "He did what?"

"He wasn't hurt," April said softly. "He lost his balance. He made us promise that we wouldn't tell anyone."

Daniel fought back a sense of disbelief. "Us?"

Kip found another chipped nail to chew. "I was there. Helped him up. He said if we'd stay quiet, he'd do his best to not work alone anymore."

Daniel scowled at his friend, then turned toward Bobby. "Did you know about this?"

Bobby shook his head. "Although Levon did tell me he thought he was getting too old to work by himself. I just thought he was talking about falling or getting hurt, not killed."

Daniel turned and stalked away, running one hand through his hair in frustration. As he passed under the arch, Ray caught his arm, speaking firmly but under his breath. "No, sir. You started this. You finish it. Your relationship with your father is not the issue."

Daniel froze, then nodded, turning back to the room. "So, again, does anyone know *why* he would have worked alone this morning?"

Bobby and Kip fell silent, but April spoke quietly. "I asked him on Sunday, when he said he planned to plow the field by himself. I got the feeling he was upset about something. I assumed it was just the drought making the corn die. Anyway, he said the plowing couldn't wait." She stared at the floor, and Daniel could almost see her going over the conversation from last Sunday in her head again.

He turned to Kip. "So do you know of any reason why he would have been upset? Anything about the crop that would've made him feel he had to plow it today, even if it meant working alone?" When his best friend shook his head, looking uncomfortable,

Daniel turned to Bobby. "You?" His cousin also shook his head.

Daniel dropped to one knee in front of the younger man. "Did you tell your mama that Dad's gone?"

Bobby nodded. "She's pretty torn up about it. Daddy had to give her one of her nerve pills to calm her down. You probably shouldn't talk to her until tomorrow about the arrangements."

Daniel nodded, then patted Bobby's knee and stood, turning to Kip. "What about Charlie?"

Kip stood. "'Bout like you'd think. We're both pretty shook."

Finally Daniel looked at Ray. "Can you think of anything else?"

The stone-faced sheriff shook his head, and Daniel escorted his friends to the door. Bobby went out first, and as Kip stepped over the threshold, he hesitated. He glanced around, then lowered his voice as he shook Daniel's hand one last time. "You should have paid more attention to what was growing in your daddy's fields, Daniel."

Daniel's grip tightened on Kip's hand. "What are you talking about?"

Kip pulled away. "You'll figure it out." He took three more steps backward, still looking at Daniel. "You'll figure it out." Then he turned and left, settling the dark red cap back on his head and tugging the bill down low over his face.

ELEVEN

When Daniel reentered the parlor, he found Aunt Suke waiting for him, two small paper bags in her hands. She pushed one at him and one at Ray. Before either could say a word, she snapped, "Ham sandwiches and chips. Take them and get out of my house."

Ray took one bag with a quiet, "Thank you, ma'am."

Daniel looked past her toward April, who still sat, head down, gaze on some distant place, on a small chair in the parlor. He raised his hand to point at her. "I just want to—"

Aunt Suke blocked his path. "No, sir. It's late. She's about to collapse and so are you. You have to stop. Now. Whatever it is can wait."

Daniel looked down in those blazing blue eyes, a flood of raw emotions churning in a confused miasma in his head. "I just want to say—"

She shook her head, her white hair flying. "No. Enough is enough. Go home."

A firm hand clutched his shoulder from behind. "She's right, Daniel. We can't do any more tonight. Jeff will take over the night watch. Let's go."

Finally he nodded, and he took the bag from Aunt Suke. "You take care of her."

"You know I will. A fluffy robe and a hot bath are waiting upstairs for her."

Silently he let Ray guide him out. He dropped the bag of food on the truck seat and headed home, suddenly grateful for the dark country night that seemed to swallow him whole.

Aunt Suke pulled April to her feet and pushed her toward the stairs. "Go up there, take a hot bath. It's already run. All you have to do is get in. I left a night-gown and guest robe on the bed. Put it on and get into bed. We'll talk more in the morning." She gave April an encouraging nudge. "Go on."

A hot bath, as it turned out, was exactly what April needed. Along with soaking away the tension in her muscles, the hot water seemed to leach out her temper and a lot of the mental stress of the day. As she slipped into the thick, fluffy robe, she relished the luxury of it.

What the bath had not relieved was the bone-deep exhaustion or the weariness that seeped through her like a stone in water, pulling her down with an oppressive weight. She took off the robe and slid in between the sheets, wanting desperately not to think of murder or anything to do with the Rivers family.

As she drifted in that twilight between wakefulness and sleep, however, the murder played again and again in her mind. Just before sleep took over, April realized that the killer's sleeves had been rolled up. His arms were white.

"So not the Reyes brothers," she murmured. White. Very white.

That night, April dreamed of a sea of red baseball

caps, floating around her, swarming her, threatening to drown her. Red caps...with a silver arc on the front.

"I know. I will." In his ear, a first cousin in Michigan sobbed openly, grief strangling her words. "I promise," he said for what felt like the one hundredth time in the past hour. "I'll keep you posted." Daniel poured the eighth cup of coffee, draining the last drop. "I'll send out an e-mail with the arrangements." He snapped off the coffeemaker and set the pot back on its perch. "Yes. I promise."

He hung up the phone, resisting the urge to throw it as hard and as far away as he could. "And that's just the *L*s."

Returning to the kitchen table, Daniel dropped heavily into the chair and ran his hand through his hair as he stared at the paperwork in front of him. Despite Ray and Aunt Suke's admonitions to sleep, Daniel knew he'd not rest easily. So, on the way home, he'd stopped by his father's house to pick up Levon's address book and the box with the important family papers. The list of people to call quickly grew to an overwhelming length, and he'd stopped when he reached the *L*s in the address book and picked up the phone. He started with the closest relatives, including Levon's remaining brother, since Bobby had already told his aunt, Levon's sister, then moved to his alphabetical list. Daniel had only paused in calling the relatives once during the last hour, in order to call Beck's, the funeral home in White Hills, grateful that someone stayed on call there all hours of the day and night.

Daniel felt as if every nerve had been sliced to the quick. Bone-weary and raw, edgy and shaking from too much caffeine, he didn't think he could stand telling one more person that his father had been killed.

He leaned back in the chair and rubbed his face. Just a few hours ago, April had shared a meal with him at this very table, a moment of peace and safety in the chaotic day. Now it was a precious diamond of a memory.

The way she'd screamed at him after the accident, the tortured look on her face broke his heart. He'd pushed too hard, put too much at risk.

They both had snapped.

What do I do now, Lord?

If he pushed again tomorrow, she might rebel completely, shutting him out.

Why do I try to bull through trouble, Lord? Even Ray has cautioned me about plowing through cases.

Daniel grimaced. Patience had never been his strong suit. But April was more than just the key witness on one of his cases. He couldn't just take charge and plow over her. She was a lady. One in trouble. One who needed all the patience and consideration he could give.

She's a lady. That's what Levon had always called Daniel's mom, and he'd treated her like one all her life.

I've been treating April like a witness, one that I was too busy interrogating to see that she is also a victim.

Daniel blew out a long breath. *Okay, tomorrow, I'll see if she'll let me apologize and start over.*

Still…frustration at making so little progress gnawed at him, and Daniel pushed the call list aside and turned to a fresh page in his notebook.

Forensics aside, this was *his* county, *his* father. *Why* would Levon get killed? *Okay…so let's start with the usual reasons for murder.*

Money? Daniel shook his head. Levon had always paid folks well, and Daniel was the only one who'd benefit financially from Levon's death, being the sole heir.

Love? No real leads there, either. Before Ray dropped him off, he'd told Daniel that he'd talked to Carla Godsey and her kids. Not only were they devastated by Levon's death, but they all had alibis for the time of the murder.

What else? Daniel drummed his fingers a moment, then froze, his thoughts latching on to one of the unusual facts of the case. The exact location. Anyone could have overheard Levon telling April last Sunday about his plans to plow…but it would take someone familiar with Levon and the layout of his fields to know exactly where to find him on his property.

So…who would know that information?

Daniel picked up the pen and started the list of names.

April, obviously.

The Reyes brothers. Most of the migrant workers hadn't yet arrived for the harvest. Julio and Antony, however, worked with his dad all summer. And he'd planned to give them that truck. Maybe they had a falling out with him? Unlikely, and Ray had cleared them.

Bobby. Levon often hired him to run the larger tractors and combines.

Kip. Same reason. Both were good with the big farm machines.

Daniel frowned at the short list. None of them were likely suspects…they had all admired and adored his dad.

Daniel's vision blurred, this time from pure exhaustion, which had overcome even the load of coffee. *I can't think. I have to sleep.*

Tomorrow, Lord. Thank You for getting us through today. Tomorrow, help me start fresh with April.

After a quick shower, Daniel stretched out on the bed, staring at the ceiling. As he drifted off, what Kip had said to him floated through his mind, confusing and out of context. Unsure of what it meant, Daniel gave himself over to sleep, but the warning followed him into his dreams.

"You should have paid more attention to what was growing in your daddy's fields, Daniel."

TWELVE

April awoke to the luring scents of bacon and biscuits, and by the time she'd grabbed the fluffy robe and headed downstairs, Aunt Suke had plates on the table. Polly munched her breakfast from a bowl next to the stove, and as April poured a cup of coffee from the pot, her hostess carried dishes of bacon, eggs, gravy and grits to the table.

"I have orange juice, if you'd like to pretend there's something healthy about this breakfast."

April laughed. "Coffee's fine. This all looks delicious. I can't believe you cooked all this for just the two of us."

"Well, I have a suspicion y'all didn't eat much yesterday, and that you've got a long day ahead. This will stick to your ribs and hold you up."

April sat and reached for a slice of bacon. "Stick to my hips, more like it."

Aunt Suke snorted. "As skinny as you are, you'd never notice." She reached into the refrigerator and drew out a dish of butter and a jar of strawberry jam that she sat in the middle of the table.

April perked up when she saw the familiar red and green label. "You buy my jams?"

"Yep, and not just because you're my neighbor. They're really good. Last Christmas I bought a bunch for those little gifts everybody hands out. Y'know, the mail carrier, the girl at the post office, my Sunday-school class."

April felt humbled, and she folded her hands in her lap. "Thank you."

Aunt Suke waved a hand at her. "Just keep making them. Now say grace before all this gets too cold to eat."

April froze. Twice in as many days, someone wanted her to say grace. "Um...I'm not very good at—"

"Don't fret over it, girl. Just talk to Him from your heart and say thanks."

It didn't leave a lot of room for argument. April closed her eyes, bowed her head and took a deep breath. "Thank You, Lord, for all this wonderful food, and everything else You've done for us." April suddenly felt a rich sense of euphoria, as if her head and heart had suddenly opened up, letting her know exactly what she needed to pray for. "And I ask You to watch over all of us, especially Daniel as he grieves and tries to work through this time. All this I ask in Your name, Amen."

When she looked up, she found that Aunt Suke's eyes glistened with tears. "So." The older woman swallowed and sat a bit straighter. "I take it you're not mad at him anymore?"

April reached for the eggs. "Sleep helped. But you knew it would, didn't you?"

"Why do you think I didn't press the subject last night?" Aunt Suke helped herself to a biscuit and sliced it open with a knife. "Anyway, I got the feeling that whatever blowup had happened, it was about what you did—or did not—remember. Too much had happened in one day. It was time to rest, let your head clear."

April crumbled bacon over her eggs, then split a biscuit and covered it in gravy. "So do I have to wait until I'm seventy to be this wise, or does it come on you gradually?"

Aunt Suke laughed, which made her look much younger. At the sound, Polly looked up, then came to lie next to Aunt Suke, scooting in under the table until her head rested on the older woman's sneakers.

"Girl, wisdom comes on you a little bit at a time, and it depends a lot on what you do with your life. I learned a lot in Korea. So did Daniel in the Middle East and Levon in Vietnam. But you don't have to serve in the military to gain a lot of it. Your sister June got a lot when she went from rebel to preacher's wife to widow."

She paused and took a sip of her coffee. "You're going to learn a lot about yourself going through this. In fact, if I'm reading you right, you already have. There's nothing like living in a pressure cooker to find out what you're made of."

April put her fork down. "You know, I go to church every Sunday, but I'm not always good at being faithful. But yesterday I heard myself tell Ray Taylor that we're not supposed to live in fear. I don't even know what part of the Bible that's in."

"Second Timothy."

April held out her hand in a "See there!" motion. "But I guess that when I heard it, it made an impact." April sat a little straighter in her chair. "All I know is that yesterday, when everyone wanted me to hide and wait, I wanted to confront. And not just because I was angry about Levon. I wanted to let everyone know that I trust God more than I fear a coward with a gun."

"Good for you."

April sighed. "But then last night, I accused Daniel of putting me at risk because he thinks I know something I don't." She told Aunt Suke about the visit to the park, more details on the accident and the blowup. "Daniel really thinks I can recognize the killer."

Aunt Suke swallowed a mouthful of grits. "No one said this would be easy, April. We just have to keep trying. And paying attention." She motioned at the robe April wore. "By the way, I have some oversize shirts you can borrow. I left them draped over a chair in your room. But my jeans would be way too short. If they won't let you back in your house, you may have to convince Daniel to take you shopping."

"If I see him."

"You will. He'll be here before you know it."

April knew her doubt showed on her face. "After last night? How can you be so sure?"

"Because he's not a man to let go of something so easily."

"That part I believe."

Aunt Suke's smile turned secretive. "Now, I want to share something. Someone told me once that you loved looking at old photos and hearing stories about times gone by."

A twinge of grief settled in April's stomach. "That would be Levon." She sighed. "His wife had put together all these albums with photos from the thirties and forties. Family stuff from both sides. They're on a bookcase in his living room, and I was constantly pulling one down and asking him about the pictures." She shrugged one shoulder. "I'm nosy like that."

Aunt Suke pushed her plate aside, then reached

down and pulled a small box from the seat of a chair next to her. The size of a large shoe box, it was dotted with small drawings of roller skates, dolls and photos. "My mother gave me this as a keepsake box for my tenth birthday. It held a lot of stuff over the years, but after she and Daddy died, I started putting the oldest pictures in it.

"I want you to take this, look through it. Most of the explanations for the pictures are written on the backs. But I especially wanted to show you this one." She pulled a snapshot out and placed it on the table.

April peered closer at it. Three men stood next to each other: Levon, Kip and Daniel. Daniel wore an army uniform, while Levon wore overalls and a work shirt and Kip had on a baseball uniform—and a red hat. All three men were laughing, heads tossed back.

"You can't tell it," Aunt Suke said, "but this was taken at the church. Daniel was home on leave, and Kip had just finished a double header at the park. Kip and Daniel were closer than brothers, but Daniel's time in the Middle East changed their relationship. He came back more serious, more determined to make something of his life."

"I figured that's why he won't go to the park to play baseball, or even watch his friends play. He can't let go of how much they've drifted apart. But Kip doesn't seem as aware of the distance. He took the news of Levon's death pretty hard."

"How hard?"

April replayed the encounter in her head. "His emotions were all over the place. One minute, he was devastated. The next, making jokes."

Aunt Suke's eyes narrowed. "Didn't that seem a little odd?"

"Uh…not really. Grieving folks can be all over the place, right? What exactly are you trying to tell me?"

Aunt Suke hesitated, then leaned back in her chair. "I refuse to put ideas in your head. If you have anything to remember—"

"I don't."

Aunt Suke nodded, but continued. "But if you do, you need to keep in mind that you're not looking for a stranger. Don't be searching the faces of everyone in the park or at church. There just aren't that many people who knew just where to find Levon, and even fewer who'd have a reason to kill him. It will be someone you've met or even talked to. It'll be someone Levon trusted enough to let him get close while carrying a shotgun."

"In other words, someone like his son's best friend."

"Someone exactly like that."

"Do you think it *is* Kip? Or Bobby?"

Aunt Suke hesitated, then finally shook her head. "It would take a mighty powerful reason for either of them to do something like this. To kill someone he loves." Aunt Suke paused. "I just think Daniel is ignoring the obvious, expecting either of them to be forthcoming with information."

April frowned. "Why wouldn't they?"

Aunt Suke let out a long sigh. "A few years ago, while Daniel was overseas, Kip got into some trouble with the law."

April leaned forward, resting her elbows on the table and focusing on Aunt Suke's face. "What for?"

The older woman shook her head. "Kip and Charlie married so young. Neither of them was ready for the responsibility. They had two kids by the time they were twenty. Charlie didn't know much about being a working mom, and Kip knew nothing about being a provider and a dad. They almost lost their home. Kip started looking for shortcuts, and he found one in pot."

April straightened. "Marijuana?"

Aunt Suke sipped her coffee, as if trying to get rid of a bad taste in her mouth. "Apparently he was involved just long enough to get into trouble. Some of the boys around here grow it out in the woods. Used to grow a lot of it, but the DEA started bring in helicopters with infrared, and it cut down on a bunch. Kip got caught in a sting."

"Did he go to jail?"

She set the cup down. "No. Ray vouched for him, and Kip turned in his dealers. Got probation. Ray and Charlie both would skin him alive if he got back into it."

"Do you think he did get back into it? Do you think Levon's death had anything to do with drugs?"

Aunt Suke sat perfectly still a moment. "I don't know. I'm asking around."

Aunt Suke fell silent again, looking down at the photo for a long time, her finger brushing across Levon's face. "Levon would never intentionally hurt a soul. So I think he made a mistake. Don't know what kind, but it must have been a doozy."

She shook her head as if to clear the memories, then pushed the photo toward April, along with the box. "Take them. Look through them. And try to think of folks who would be familiar with Levon's schedule."

Polly sat up suddenly, a low rumble in her throat. After a few seconds, however, the rumble turned to a gentle whine, and the shepherd trotted toward the front door.

"Must be Daniel."

April put down her fork. "Yikes! I'm not dressed." She stood up and headed back toward her room, tucking the box under her arm. Behind her, Aunt Suke mumbled something about young people, but April ignored her. She had so much she wanted to tell Daniel this morning—she hoped he wasn't still mad.

Start with an apology, then tell him about the dream. April flung the robe on the bed, put on the bulletproof vest, then grabbed one of the loaner shirts Aunt Suke had left for her and slipped on her jeans. April started to head for the door, but a last-minute check in the mirror stopped her. She plucked at the shirt, which was so big it was uncomfortable, and wondered how Aunt Suke wore them this large.

Definitely need to go shopping. Accepting that this was the best she could do, April headed for the stairs.

Daniel waited at the bottom, hat in hand. As April's foot hit the last step, they both spoke, almost in unison.

"April—"

"Daniel—"

"I'm sor—"

"I'm sorry—"

Both stopped for a second, waiting and a little wary, and Aunt Suke stepped from behind Daniel. "Well, now that that's out of the way, you two get out of my house so I can get some work done. Can't play hostess forever."

As she passed April on the stairs, she nudged her forward. "Go on. Git." She paused and looked back at Daniel. "And I'm serious, young man, either get her into her house or get her into Springfield for some clothes. She looks like a ragamuffin in my old shirt."

Eyes wide with embarrassment, April stared at Aunt Suke. "I don't believe you told him—"

Aunt Suke's eyes glittered with amusement. "Let him take care of you. He needs to buy you some clothes."

"He does not!"

Aunt Suke fluttered both hands at them wildly. "You two are harder to get rid of than a flock of blackbirds. Go on!"

Daniel held out his hand. "Ms. Presley? We'd better leave before she sics Polly on us."

With an exaggerated sigh, April took it. "You're right, Mr. Rivers."

Muttering under her breath about sassy children, Aunt Suke headed up the stairs, and April and Daniel turned toward the door. As he opened it, April looked up at him, "But you really don't owe me anything."

He shut the door. "Except an apology." He paused on the porch and squeezed her hand. "That fit yesterday was uncalled-for. And I'm sorry. I just couldn't believe I was such an idiot about calling Kip and Bobby over to the truck."

April returned the squeeze, cherishing how warm and strong his hand felt in hers. "I was scared, too."

He touched her cheek lightly. "Thank you."

She nodded and they got in the black truck. Daniel settled and put on his seat belt but didn't start the engine. After a moment, April touched his arm. "Are you okay?"

He nodded and looked up at her. "I didn't mean to push so hard yesterday. I know that memories of something as traumatic as a murder can be triggered, but I also know they can't be forced. I was out of line, and I also never took into consideration that you might not remember anything, that there might not be anything to be triggered at all."

April looked down at her hands in her lap for a moment, then took a deep breath to steady her nerves. "He was white."

Daniel sat quite still. "What?"

April's mind spun through the remembrances of the night before. "When I got home, I took a hot bath, then went to bed. It all relaxed me, I guess. As I started to go to sleep, there were these…flashes."

Daniel gripped the steering wheel tightly, staring at the dashboard. "What did you see?"

Her fingers quivered, and April clutched them together. "His shirtsleeves were rolled up. He was white." She looked up at Daniel. "Too white to be one of the migrant workers, including Julio and Antony."

Daniel looked up at her. "You're sure?"

She nodded. "And there was something on the hat."

His eyes widened. "What?"

She pointed to her forehead, drawing a circle in the air with her forefinger. "It was silver, or maybe white. Just one color. Rounded, like an *O* or a cursive *A*." She hesitated. "Or the top of an arc."

This time, his eyes narrowed. "Like a rainbow? That kind of arc?"

April stared back at her hands, her mind on the memory. "I think so." She looked up again. "But I couldn't swear to it. It's still too much like something I dreamed."

Daniel nodded slowly. "Anything else?"

She shook her head. "Just that I'm really sorry for screaming at you. You were right. I just didn't want to admit it. I really didn't think that—"

"People don't understand." Daniel's soft words were almost soothing in tone. "Seeing a murder is never as clear and clean-cut as they make it out to be on television. Your mind doesn't want to accept what you've seen. It's a kind of perceptual blindness. You can be looking straight at a killing, from only a few feet away, and not be able to immediately recall details. It's even worse if it's someone…" His words faltered.

"Someone you love," she finished.

He nodded. "You focus on the person you care about and what's happening *to* them instead of what's happening *around* them. Just as when we first talked, and all you could remember was—"

"Seeing Levon get shot." April's hands now felt like blocks of ice.

"But it's a fragile time. You may or may not start to recall details, but you also may not accept that your memories are real. So if you wait too long, you'll think you've either imagined them or forget them entirely."

She looked up at him. "You think I'll remember the silver thing more clearly."

He nodded slowly. "If you see it in the right context."

"Will I ever remember a face?"

He shrugged one shoulder and looked out over the hood of the truck, his gaze on some far horizon. "Possibly, but clothes, hats—those are things that don't shift. His face was probably angry, changing and at a distance, probably a little blurry with movement."

April watched his face a moment, the tension in his jaw, the faraway gaze. "Is that what happened to you in Iraq?"

Silence hovered between them a moment. Then he reached for the keys and started the engine. "Yes." He put the truck in Reverse.

"Where are we going?"

"The station. Ray wants to see you about something." He held up his hand as she opened her mouth. "No, I don't know about what."

As they drove, April felt a lot of her energy, a lot of her drive truly returning. The dreams had encouraged her spirit, almost reassuring her that she could, in fact, play a part in solving Levon's murder. She closed her eyes, feeling the sun on her face, knowing she could embrace the day.

Beneath her breath, April began to hum, not realizing even what the tune was until Daniel began to sing harmony on the hymn "Unclouded Day." She grinned at him, almost laughing as they finished the song together. Shifting a bit in her seat, April rested her hand on his shoulder, where she left it until he turned the big truck into a parking space in front of the station.

Daniel got out first and checked the area carefully before opening the door and escorting her into the station. Per Ray's instructions, he led her to the sheriff's office and closed the door.

Ray's office, a purely utilitarian room holding only a desk, one set of shelves and three chairs, overlooked the parking lot behind the station. Standing behind the desk, Ray held out a set of keys.

Daniel and April looked at each other, puzzled, then back at the sheriff. Ray grimaced with the expression of a man acting against his better nature. "Aunt Suke," he said evenly, "is on a mission." He shook the keys.

Daniel took them. "What are you talking about?"

Ray let out a long, exasperated sigh. "You came in the front door in the truck. Just in case you're being followed this bright and early morning, you'll go out the back. Just outside the door is a gray Toyota." He nodded at the keys. "It was my wife's. I've kept it up, but it's been in the garage since she died three years ago. It won't be noticeable or recognizable. And the windows are tinted."

April blinked, still puzzled. "Where are we going?"

"Backroads to Springfield. Aunt Suke called Betty Woods and asked her to open up her shop two hours early. You'll go in through the back alley."

"You're joking."

Ray shook his head. "Aunt Suke is determined to get you some new clothes, even if we have to play some idiotic spy game to do it."

April looked at Daniel. "We don't have to. I can cope."

"No doubt." He glanced sideways at her. "But to be brutally honest, there's something a little disconcerting about you looking and smelling like Aunt Suke's closet."

April blinked once, surprised at his words, then she sniffed her sleeve. Mothballs. And she hadn't even noticed.

She did notice, however, the slight mischievous grin on Daniel's face, and she laughed. "Okay. We'll shop."

Ray growled. "And would you tell that old woman I'm not James Bond in disguise!"

Daniel leaned against the back door of the small dress shop in Springfield, watching April's progress. Betty's Boutique didn't open until noon on Saturdays, so the front shades were still down, the front door securely locked. He had to give Aunt Suke credit. In terms of a safe place to buy clothes, it didn't get much better. The little gray car in the alley almost blocked the back door, and unless they had been seen getting out of it, the nondescript vehicle would not have been associated with either of them.

As they had left the station, Ray told him that he'd leave the truck in front for a couple of hours, then take it to the body shop. *We might just pull this off. A free morning.* Ray had several things to follow up on in the investigation and had strongly suggested that Daniel and April stay far out of his way for most of the day. After the dress shop, Daniel planned to get takeout and head for a private lake for a little while, just to talk.

For now, however, he watched April shop. He *liked* watching her shop. Just shopping for a couple of new shirts and a pair of jeans seemed to make her a bit more lighthearted.

It had been a rough twenty-four hours. Daniel still had trouble remembering that his father was dead, that he'd never see him again, even though he'd called the remaining relatives that morning before heading to Aunt Suke's. Everyone's shock and disbelief resonated with him. He could barely believe it himself.

Watching April helped, in an odd way, and he finally understood why Levon had wanted to see April and him make a go of it.

Turning to check the back door again, he found himself wondering if April realized that Levon had thought they would make a good couple. He still remembered a chat he'd had with his father about it, trying to explain that April had turned him down.

"She's just not interested, Dad."

"Oh, yes, she is. She's just not ready yet."

"Isn't that the same thing?"

"*Not interested means never. Not ready means hang tight and wait.*"

But he'd never asked her out again.

Daniel straightened and prowled the shop again, peering cautiously around the shades on the door, as April carried the clothes to the cashier's counter. Excellent.

Daniel scanned the street one more time. He'd taken the narrowest, curviest back road possible from Caralinda into Robertson County and Springfield, hoping to discourage anyone from following them. He hadn't spotted anyone, but wasn't taking any chances. Whoever wanted April dead had stayed right with them yesterday, and Daniel truly hoped their ruse today had made a difference.

He hoped April would remember more, or that Ray's investigation would reveal something that would bring this to a quick end. What was true in the city was also true in small towns: if a killer isn't caught in the first forty-eight hours, chances of solving the crime dwindle by the hour.

Which made Daniel second-guess holding back information from his boss. After April had pulled the first clothes from the racks and he'd secured the back door, Daniel had called Ray to tell him that April had confirmed the killer's race, but not what she'd told him about the cap. He'd told himself the information had too many uncertainties about it. Could be silver, could be white. Could be an arc, an *O,* or some circular design. There were just too many unknowns to make it useful.

Daniel turned from the front door and crossed his arms. He had to admit, however, that it would be too easy for him to assume that when she said it looked like a silver rainbow, she hadn't imagined or mistaken anything.

A silver *O,* breaking open on the right side to be transformed into a stylized rainbow with one leg of the bow shorter than the other had been the logo on the work caps for the now-defunct Orion Materials. Located over in Sumner County, Orion had been out of business for quite a while, and, even when it had been in business, only six or seven men in Caralinda had worked there.

Daniel let out a long breath, hoping he'd made the right choice, since one of those men, and the only one who'd been in Levon Rivers's life, was Kip Redding.

THIRTEEN

"This is gorgeous." April's whispery words blended well with the gentle breeze that moved over the small blue lake in front of them.

"It's an advantage of spending almost thirty years in the same county. Friends with land."

This was private property, complete with a gate at the end of the road, but Daniel had parked under a tree with low-hanging branches, half facing the road and the lake.

April dug a packet of fries out of the take-out bag and handed it to him. "Who owns this place?"

He shrugged. "Army buddy. He bought this place in case there's a total collapse in society. Lots of water, easy to supply and fortify."

April froze, a burger half out of the bag. "You're kidding me, right?"

Daniel shook his head and popped a fry into his mouth. "Nope."

"That's crazy."

"But he's a real nice guy."

April snorted a laugh. "So we're safe."

He reached for the burger. "At this moment, we'd need a bunker to be safer."

She let out a long sigh. "Feels nice."

"Oh, yeah." Daniel dug into his food with gusto, but April plucked only at a few French fries, lost in thought. He watched her a few minutes before asking, "Not hungry or not good?"

She looked up at him, startled. "What?"

He pointed at her still-wrapped burger. "I would have thought after this morning's clothing safari you would have been starved."

April tried to wave away his concern. "No, it's good. You should have seen the breakfast Aunt Suke cooked this morning."

But that wasn't all. He could see it in her eyes. "Still, I would have thought you worked that off just changing clothes half a million times."

She grimaced sharply and put the burger back in the bag, and he knew he'd hit home. "April, talk to me. What's wrong?"

She couldn't look at him. "It just doesn't seem right."

"What?"

Her hand fluttered as if she were trying to pull the right words out of the air. "The shopping."

He got it. "You mean, it seems awful for us to be singing and laughing and buying clothes when my father is in the morgue and some lunatic wants to kill you?"

Her head snapped up, eyes blazing with irritation and glistening with tears. "You certainly don't pull punches."

Daniel dropped his burger and shifted in his seat to face her fully. "April, listen to me. Have you ever lost someone close to you?"

She hesitated, then lowered her gaze to her lap. "My mother. A long time ago."

"Then you know it hurts." He paused, grimacing at a sudden memory of his dad that his words brought out. "Believe me, it hurts. I haven't forgotten that my dad is dead. It's an unbelievably painful wound, like someone tried to rip my heart out.

"But we all handle it differently. Sometimes the very details that have to be handled keep us going for a few days, keeping us afloat when all we really want to do is curl up in a ball and grieve. We have to go on."

He gripped her hands tightly, trying to give her an anchor. "And yesterday morning, you stepped onto the most unbelievable roller coaster life could ever throw at someone. Not only did you lose a best friend, but you saw him murdered. You got snatched up in the investigation. And you had me dragging you all over creation, *making* you think about it. Truthfully, I'm surprised you're still talking to me!"

Daniel took a deep breath. "Don't beat yourself up for laughing, for taking some joy in normality. It's a way of coping with the maelstrom you're in. It doesn't mean you've forgotten Dad or that you're not hurting. It means you're human and you're trying to survive."

Two tears slid from the corners of her eyes. "Aunt Suke warned me that I was about to learn a lot about myself."

Daniel released one hand and wiped away the tears with his finger. "If you're the woman I think you are, you learn something every day. After all, you went through a horrific divorce. You don't go through something like that without learning a lot about yourself, about grief and healing."

April's eyes narrowed at that comment, and she studied him a few moments, a pensive expression on her face. "You've been watching me?"

It was a punch to the gut, and Daniel released her hands and sat back, heat flooding his face. "Actually," he said quietly, "I've been waiting on you."

April's face softened. "I thought that when I turned you down last year, you'd just move on. I'd even asked Levon who you were seeing."

"If you expected me to move on, why did you care who I was seeing?"

It was April's turn to blush, and her hand flew to her cheek. "Well, I mean, turning you down wasn't about *you,* it was because I still needed to get past some things, and, after all, you're a good-looking guy, who— Oop!" The hand covered her mouth, and the flush in her cheeks spread across the rest of April's face.

Daniel fought the urge to laugh, and an odd sense of relief washed over him as he realized he wasn't alone in his interest. Instead he said something he knew she needed to hear.

"Dad told me to wait on you."

April's hands fell to her lap again. "He did?"

Daniel nodded. "He knew. He saw as soon as I did what kind of woman you are, that we could be happy together." As he watched the truth of his statement sink in for her, Daniel made up his mind about something. "When we get through here, I want to show you something."

Every morning, Levon Rivers had microwaved four slices of bacon and baked five canned biscuits for breakfast. The scents of both permanently permeated his house, leaving it with a welcoming feel of a well-loved home.

April stood in the femininely decorated living room

and sniffed. "Do you think we'll ever come here without expecting to see him at the table?"

Daniel checked the window and front door locks and closed all the blinds. He'd parked the gray car in the garage behind the house, and they had come in through the back door. "Probably not."

April looked around at the familiar room, a hollow ache in her chest. "What will you do?"

He shrugged as he walked toward a pie safe in the kitchen. "Probably nothing for a while. Dad had several offers from housing developers, but he once told me that he'd hate to see the land go that way."

"He mentioned once that he'd love to see it belong to Caralinda."

Daniel pulled a photo album from the safe and motioned for April to sit on the living room couch. "That's a strong possibility, once everything has been cleared up."

April sat. "Another reason to wait for a while."

He nodded and joined her. "I know you've looked at a lot of Dad's photo albums. Have you seen this one?"

April looked closely at the leather-bound volume that Daniel held carefully on his lap. "No. Not that one. What is it?"

He opened the cover and shifted so that they shared the weight of it. "The story of Levon and Maddie Rivers."

April felt a rush of anticipation. "Show me."

Grinning, he turned a page. "My mother put this together not long after they got married, then added to it a little each year. She had lots of albums that showed us as a family, but this is just about them. She once told me that it was to remind her that her priorities were

God, husband, family, work, in that order. That if you mix up that order, everything goes out of whack."

The first page of the album showed Maddie and Levon as schoolkids in the forties and teenagers in the fifties. Her rich brown hair, slick and short as a girl, poofed into vivacious curls as she entered her late teens. Levon, his Native American ancestry shining through his high cheekbones and smooth, dark hair, looked like a 1950s Hollywood star.

Daniel turned the page to reveal a wedding photo. Maddie gleamed in a white satin gown, while Levon looked stern and reserved in an Army uniform.

"Wow," April whispered.

"Yeah," Daniel agreed. "Vietnam. They got married after my father was drafted, sometime between boot camp and him shipping out." He paused. "Mother told me that for a long time, she wasn't quite sure that had been the right thing to do."

April looked up sharply. "Why?"

He turned the page and pointed to a photo of Levon and Maddie at a picnic table. They sat facing opposite directions. Maddie, in a conservative dress and well-combed hair, made a stark contrast to a hippielike Levon, whose long hair was out of control and streaked with gray. Smoke curled from a hand-rolled cigarette in his right hand. "A friend took this to show them how far apart they'd grown."

Daniel leaned back against the couch. "My father returned from Vietnam an entirely different man. Mother once told me that it was like living with a stranger. He was struggling with his faith, dabbling in drugs... That wasn't a regular cigarette in his hand. Mom told me it was a marijuana joint. After this picture was made, they realized they had to either go their separate ways or start from scratch."

"They started from scratch."

He nodded. "All the way back to the first date. He moved into the spare bedroom, and they vowed not to see or talk to each other outside of the way they would as a courting couple. Dates. Ball games. Concerts. Dad stopped smoking pot and tobacco, and made peace with God again. Mother let her hair grow. He introduced her to rock music, and she reminded him of how much he liked bluegrass."

He turned another page and pointed to another wedding photo, this one on a beach. Maddie looked more relaxed, and Levon looked like he'd found his roots again.

"They remarried?"

"Yep, even though they'd never divorced. They wanted to celebrate how they'd found each other again. This was 1978. I was born the next year."

April smiled at him. "You're telling me you come from a very patient family."

He laughed. "And a family of people who have their priorities straight." He reached up and cupped her chin with his hand. "When you know what's right, you're willing to wait for it."

His soft kiss grew firmer as April slid her hand behind his neck and a sweet, aching longing washed over her like a warm, comforting river. Daniel was right—they had both been waiting for her to heal, for the time to be right. And this felt more *right* than anything April had felt in a long time.

As their lips parted, April let out a long sigh. "Wow."

Daniel's eyes sparkled with humor. "Thanks. Glad you liked it."

April laughed. "You're welcome."

Daniel closed the photo album and put his hand flat on the cover. "I should warn you. This is what I want for my life. Two people going in the same direction."

April's eyes widened as her throat tightened, making her words hoarse. "I will consider myself warned."

From upstairs, an ancient clock chimed five, breaking the awkward moment. Daniel checked his watch, then set the album aside on the couch. He stood and took April's hand. "C'mon. I want to show you another bit of my father's legacy."

She stood. "What?"

He led the way to the door. "You'll see. And it might even spur a few more of those memories locked in your head." He stopped and turned to her. "No. Maybe not."

"Why not?"

"Too risky. Too uncontrolled. It might put you out in the open too much."

"We could ask Aunt Suke for James Bond scenarios."

He stared at her, eyes wide and bright, although she couldn't tell if the gleam was from humor or annoyance.

"April, this is serious."

"And if I remember correctly, he's shooting at me. Shouldn't I have a say? Like I told you yesterday, I won't stay in hibernation. I won't live in fear. Plus, I'm still wearing the vest." She squeezed his hand. "You gave me a beautiful, *safe* day, and I'm grateful for that. But I can't hide forever. You have an idea that this could help me remember, more than the park did. So let's do what has to be done."

Daniel took a deep breath. "Then welcome back to reality," he muttered as the door closed behind them.

FOURTEEN

"This will show you another side of the good citizens of Caralinda."

Saturday nights meant bluegrass in Caralinda, and by five-thirty, the parking lot of the Caralinda Recreation Center overflowed with an assortment of pickups, SUVs and late-model cars. The sun, dropping low on the horizon, cast long shadows as folks mingled and called to each other. Quite a few of the trucks and SUVs had impromptu parties going on around them, complete with portable grills, coolers and lawn chairs.

"Caralinda's version of tailgating," Daniel explained as he passed the main parking lot. "I can't believe you've been here a year and haven't come out for the mingling, food and music."

Eyes wide with wonder, April took in the movable feast of the parking-lot clusters. "Your dad invited me a couple of times, but I do most of my week's order processing and marketing on Saturdays. By suppertime, I'm too tired to think, much less go out."

"See? You didn't know what you were missing."

"I do see."

Daniel pulled the little gray car into the narrow,

secluded driveway behind the center. "This is the musicians' entrance. There's an elevated walking track around the main hall, which will give us some cover. We're going to sit in the far corner underneath it. Once the lights are down for the music, it's pretty dark under the track. No one will be able to see you more than a few feet away."

Daniel moved quickly down the inside wall of the hall, but word had spread throughout the town about Levon, and a lot of the folks spotted Daniel and wanted to offer condolences and help. The women hugged him and promised to bring food. Men grabbed his hand and told him what a great guy his dad had been.

By the time they reached the back corner, a weary look had shaded Daniel's eyes, and April got an inkling of exactly how rough Levon's funeral was going to be. *I'll be with you,* she promised silently, wishing she knew how to tell him out loud.

Instead she pressed close to his side and squeezed his arm again. "It'll be okay. Let's sit."

He nodded and led her to the far table, where they both sat, backs against the wall, as the lights went down. The hall, a cavernous structure with basketball goals, a polished wooden floor and concrete walls, wasn't exactly an acoustic paradise, but the music made up only part of the equation. This was more like a dinner on the grounds with music than a real concert or dance.

This was about Caralinda. About community.

Daniel leaned close to her, speaking into her ear. "Aunt Suke paid for this building, but my dad was the one who started booking the bands and asking people to come. No charge. After a while, the city started asking for donations to continue it, and it's been self-sustaining for several years now."

I gotta get out more. April found herself a bit annoyed that she'd ignored Levon's invitations, had kept to herself so much.

But I needed the time.

Patience.

April watched Daniel. He certainly had it, which she had not suspected yesterday. She realized now that a lot of his behavior yesterday centered around his loss, not his true personality. Everyone grieves in their own way.

Inside the hall, no grieving showed. The party cooked on all burners. At one end, a four-piece band— guitar, mandolin, fiddle and bass—showed all signs of bringing the house down with vibrant bluegrass tunes. Around the hall, friends and families grouped around tables, sharing food and fellowship. Kids darted to and fro, their wild giggles and squeals adding a lively school-yard atmosphere to the room, which made April grin.

Daniel leaned close to April again. "So what do you think?"

"I love it. I guess I was expecting a dance."

He chuckled. "Are you kidding? Most of these raw-boned boys do well to cross the fields without tripping over their own boots."

She looked at him in surprise. "Don't most play some kind of sport?"

He nodded, his gaze sweeping the room. "Yeah, but that's different. Most of these guys never left the eighth grade when it comes to dancing with girls, even their wives." At that moment, he spotted Kip, who had a lovely, petite woman in her late twenties in tow. "I'll be right back. I want you to meet Charlie." Daniel stood and motioned at the pair.

April blanked for a moment on the name, then remembered Charlie was Kip's wife. *I have to work on my short-term memory.* April heard the woman call out Daniel's name, then the three of them came together, Charlie hugging Daniel with warmth and condolence. Charlie, also blond but with a long ponytail streaming down her back, looked much younger than her age, even though April knew they were all born the same year.

Charlie let go of Daniel and grabbed one of April's hands. "You must be April. Levon talked a lot about you, and I know I've seen you at church. I wish we'd met sooner."

"Me, too," was all April could manage.

Kip punched Daniel lightly in the arm. "Didn't think you'd make it tonight. With what's going on and all."

Daniel sat down, scooting his chair closer to April, taking her hand. "I wanted to show April another side of Caralinda."

Kip nodded. "This'll do it. Welcome to the party side."

Charlie scowled momentarily at her husband as they both pulled up chairs and sat at the table. "You make it sound like a frat house." She looked back at April, scrunching her nose as a sign of disapproval toward Kip. "Ignore him. This is a family time. It's city property. No booze. Daniel and his friends make sure it's safe for the kids."

"Speaking of," Daniel said, "where are Caylie and Aaron?"

Kip gave a look of mock astonishment. "We still have kids? We haven't really seen them since they got 'too old' to hang out with their parents."

Charlie gave Kip a playful swat. "I'm so glad to meet you!" she said to April. "You have to come over sometime soon. Daniel and Bobby are in and out of our house all the time. I usually keep cake in the fridge for company, so we could have cake and coffee and just girl chat. It would be a good break from just having the guys around."

"Hey, I thought you kept that cake around for me!"

"Hush."

April bit her lip to keep from grinning. *These two are like teenagers on caffeine.*

Kip put his arm around Charlie, but spoke to Daniel. "So are you here for the music or on the case?"

Daniel looked around at the band, which had just launched into an upbeat rendition of "Let It Shine," and April could see the longing in his eyes. "Both."

"Excellent. Y'all stay put, and we'll get a plate of hot dogs from one of the cooks outside. Sit tight."

Daniel remained seated, his eyes scanning the faces in the crowd.

"You're working, aren't you?"

Still focused on the people, he smiled slightly. "I still have to keep you safe. And, yes, I'd like to have a feel for who all is here."

"So do you know everyone in Caralinda?"

"Pretty much. Ray tries to keep officers in the county assigned to the areas where they live. That way we get to know folks, know who makes trouble and why." Daniel glanced at her briefly. "He used to joke about us being 'embedded' in the community. I live closer to

White Hills, but I grew up here, went to school here. Almost everyone under forty is someone I remember from school or the kid of one."

"So you seldom meet a stranger."

"Not usually. If I do, I take time to introduce myself, give them my card."

"Look in their eyes."

His grin broadened. "You'd be amazed what the eyes can reveal."

"I'm learning."

"Food!" Kip set four soft drinks on the table, then slid into the chair next to April, giving her a playful nudge. Charlie, carrying the hot dogs, sat next to him.

"Careful he doesn't disappear into the music," Kip said. "He can get carried away when he's listening to a band. Forgets the rest of the world is here. You might have to nudge him sometimes."

"Ignore him," Daniel responded. "Kip's too self-absorbed to lose himself in anything but his own ego."

"And they both think they're funnier than they really are."

April looked over at Charlie, and both women laughed.

The banter and the music continued for another hour or so, until Kip looked at his watch and tapped Charlie on the shoulder. "Gotta go, folks," he said.

"What's up?" Daniel asked.

"Gotta cook breakfast in the morning for the men's group. Six in the morning on a Sunday. What was I thinking?"

"That it was a good thing to do," said Charlie. She tugged at his sleeve. "C'mon, husband. Time to head for the homestead."

Kip reached for April's hand and kissed it with exaggerated gallantry. "My dear lady, it was very nice to spend the evening with you."

Daniel reached over and removed April's hand from Kip's grasp. "Go home."

Kip saluted Daniel, then paused, his eyes suddenly, unexpectedly somber. "Don't forget what I said." Kip then turned and followed his wife from the hall.

April, startled by the change in mood, looked at Daniel. "What did that mean?"

He shook his head once. "I don't know. Kip can be a little hard to follow." Daniel's smile held a touch of sadness. "He's a goof, but he's a terrific dad and a great husband."

"A good friend."

Daniel smiled, then turned his attention to the band as they hit the bridge of a Ralph Stanley tune.

The song ended, and the lead singer stepped to the mike to announce a fifteen-minute break. As the performers left the stage and people began milling about more chaotically, calling to friends or in search of food and drinks, April felt her unease grow, and she turned to Daniel. "Daniel, would you mind if we went back to Aunt Suke's?"

Daniel looked at her, concern on his face. "Is it too much?"

She hesitated, then nodded. "I love the music, but with all these people, I think I'm more nervous than I am focused on anything I might remember."

"Sure." He stood and offered her his hand, leading her down the side wall and out the back door.

Even though they had escaped the crowd, April's apprehension abruptly grew stronger. She felt exposed, vulnerable, and she tightened her grip on Daniel's hand as he moved toward the car, the keys in his opposite hand. He reached to shove the key in the door lock, but it stopped short, skidded away from the lock and down the door, leaving a harsh scratch in the paint.

"Daniel!" April gasped.

Daniel muttered under his breath, trying the key again. It wouldn't go in the lock. "It's jammed." He turned and grabbed her, pushing her toward the ground. "Get down! Get under the car!"

She hit the ground, the concrete scouring her hands, as Daniel pulled his gun, using the butt to break the window of the car. Before he could get the door open, however, the shots rang out, three in succession.

Daniel crouched behind the car, but the last shot ricocheted wildly off the center's brick wall, and April heard Daniel's grunt and a sharp intake of air.

She looked up, just in time to see Daniel tense and his body jerk lightly, like a marionette. A dark red stain exploded on his shirt, rapidly spreading from his shoulder down across his chest. Daniel's knees buckled and he sank to the ground, his eyes on her.

The next thing April heard were the screams that followed, including one she knew was her own.

FIFTEEN

"You may have saved his life, putting pressure on the wound like that." Ray Taylor focused on the twisting road, steering his heavy cruiser expertly through the tight turns and curves.

On the passenger side, April stared at her hands and the bunched paper towels someone had given her as the EMTs had loaded Daniel into the ambulance. Splotches of sticky, drying blood coated the towels, along with her hands and arms.

Daniel's blood.

Ray continued explaining, and April let the words roll over her, realizing it was his way of dealing with the shooting, his attempt to comfort her. "It hit his shoulder, but probably too low for a major artery. A clean hit, one that he'll probably recover from quickly."

She plucked at one of the sticky towels. *Wonder how much he lost.*

"The EMTs saw no reason to LifeFlight him to Vandy. NorthCrest Medical is very good. They have a major E.R. facility and handle about thirty thousand patients a year, including trauma cases. They know what they're doing."

April finally spoke, her words almost lost in the roar

of the cruiser's engine. "Why would anyone do this? Why would you kill someone you cared about?"

"They weren't aiming for him, April. They were aiming for you. It was a ricochet. Just his shoulder. He'll be okay, April. I promise. Daniel's not dead."

She looked up at him. "I know, but Levon is." She ground her teeth in rage and frustration. "He shot Daniel because of Levon. And me. Whoever pulled the trigger knew all of us!"

"You got that right." Ray glanced at her, the lights of an oncoming car casting harsh shadows of light and dark on his chiseled face. "And it's hard to think of anyone we know being this kind of killer."

"Anyone we know."

Kip. April took a deep breath. She should tell him Aunt Suke's suspicions.

But he's the sheriff. Surely he's been down that road, too, figuring out who would know Levon's schedule, and who among the few people had criminal records already. He had to have already considered Kip.

Motive. Murder was more than opportunity, it was also about motive. *What possible motive would Kip have?*

"He's a goof, but he's a terrific dad and a great husband."

"A good friend."

April looked down at her hands again, clutching her fingers together. *And what would such an accusation do to a good man? Especially one who had been in trouble before.* No. It could wait. There was no evidence, no connection to the murder, no apparent motive. Just Aunt Suke's suspicion that Kip would be the most likely suspect given his problems in the past. Conjecture. That's all. It would have to wait.

"April?"

She looked up again.

"Have you remembered anything important?"

"He told you about the hat?" April knew Daniel had called Ray while she shopped.

Ray nodded. "Yes."

"And the silver arc?" April stared at Ray's suddenly frozen features and knew Daniel had left that part out. *Why would he do that?*

Ray's words fell hard on her ears. "Tell me about that silver arc."

"It's a logo on the front of the hat." She stumbled over the next words. "He probably didn't tell you because I don't remember many details. It's white or silver. Roundish, like an *O* or a cursive *A*."

"Or a rainbow?"

April closed her eyes. A rainbow. Daniel and Ray both had latched on to that. It must mean something. "Yes, but I don't remember it clearly."

"Do you think you could draw it?"

She looked up, curious. "Draw it?"

He nodded, once, sharply. "When things calm down a bit, just try it. See what you can remember."

"I could try."

Maybe it shouldn't wait. "Ray."

"Talk to me."

"Does Kip have a hat with a logo like that?"

Ray hesitated. "He might. Why do you ask?"

"Aunt Suke thinks it might be Kip."

Ray's jaw tightened, but he didn't respond. They fell silent as the streets of Springfield opened up before them, and Ray slowed the cruiser, turning onto Tom Austin Highway, then into the NorthCrest Medical

Center complex. April could see the ambulance that had carried Daniel near the E.R. entrance, the doors still open.

She followed Ray through the waiting area, where he identified himself and explained that Daniel was his deputy. Spotting the blood on April, the girl behind the desk focused on her.

"Are you hurt, honey?"

April swallowed hard. "No. It's his blood. Daniel's."

The girl, whose sweet face and manner offset the professional wariness in her eyes, nodded. "We'll get you in a room so you can clean up, too. It's a pretty slow night." She looked at Ray. "But you'll have to stay here until someone can talk to you."

A few minutes later, April stood in an examining room, dropping the now-sticky paper towels into a waste hamper while a nurse watched. "You don't have to stay if you're busy. I'm just going to wash."

The nurse shook her head. "Gotta make sure you're not the next patient. That none of that is yours."

After she finished, the nurse insisted April sit for a moment before returning to the waiting room. Too weak to argue, April sat.

It was too much. Levon dead. Her home destroyed. Daniel shot. *Lord, how can life go so wrong so quickly? Please help Daniel. Please help us.*

Alone, finally away from curious eyes, demanding investigators and people who wanted to kill her, April Presley wept.

"The Lord looked out for your deputy, Sheriff Taylor." The E.R. physician crossed his arms over his chest. "The bullet exited cleanly, touched nothing vital."

For more than two hours, Ray and April had wanted to hear this news, both of them impatient and cranky in the waiting room. "So he'll be okay?" Ray asked.

The doctor nodded. "He's lost a lot of blood, and there may be some nerve damage. We cleaned the wound and patched what we needed to. They're moving him into a room now, so it'll still be a while before you can see him. I want to keep him at least a couple of days, make sure there's no infection and that he's healing properly. He'll be sore for a few weeks and the arm will be weak for maybe six months. But he'll make a full recovery."

"When can we see him?"

The doctor looked at April. "You need sleep. I've heard what you went through—"

April waved away his concern. "I really want to see him."

"Although we didn't have to do any kind of major surgery, we dosed him pretty good for the pain. He'll be asleep for several hours, if not all night, Ms. Presley."

April grabbed the doctor's arm. "You don't understand. He took a bullet for me. I'm not leaving."

Six hours later, April awoke for the seventh time as the nurse came in to check on Daniel. She shifted in the recliner next to his bed, stretching stiff muscles beneath her blanket as she watched the nurse inject fluid into the IV port. "What's that?" Her voice, clogged with sleep and weariness, could barely be heard, and she cleared her throat.

The nurse finished, dropped the needle in the biohazard box on the wall near the door and crossed back to April, squatting next to the recliner. "Just an antibiotic against infection and a painkiller. He'll probably sleep a few more hours." The nurse, a pleasant-faced woman in her forties, reached into the pocket of her scrubs and pulled out a bottle. "I brought you some water. There's more at the nurses' station, and some snacks. If you need anything, just ask."

April took the water, smiling gratefully. "Thank you."

The nurse patted her arm. "I go off in a few, but the morning nurse knows your situation. We're all pulling for you, honey."

"For me?"

She nodded. "For both of you. Word's spreading pretty quick about what happened. We think it's great that you stayed."

"Wow. I appreciate your telling me."

The nurse squeezed April's shoulder as she stood. "Hang in there. And try to get some rest." She left, the door closing behind her with a soft wisp.

"Rest," she whispered. She'd tried, without much success. A hospital wasn't really conducive to uninterrupted sleep, even for the patients. *Caring for people,* April decided, *is a noisy business.*

Pushing the blanket aside, she stood, stretching again. Even though she'd slept reasonably well at Aunt Suke's, now April felt as if she'd not slept in a month. Weariness clogged her mind and ran deep into her bones.

"But nothing like you're going through, huh?" she whispered to the unconscious Daniel. She moved closer to the bed, examining ever detail of his face. "At least you're looking better." When she'd first walked in, April had been stunned at how gray and sallow he looked, almost as if he weren't truly still alive. A thick, efficient dressing covered his shoulder and tubes ran from the veins in each arm. Over his head, one IV bag held a clear fluid, the other, the dark red nourishment of blood. He'd received his last pint at midnight, and now his skin flushed a healthier rose under the half-grown beard.

She closed her hand over his, cherishing the warmth that she found there. Before, his hands and feet had been icy from the loss of blood, and the nurses had piled thick blankets across the bed. Now, most of those had been removed, and Daniel looked as if he'd wake up any moment.

"I'm so glad," she whispered. "I'm glad you were there. Glad you're here. I don't want to be without you."

And it was true. In just two days, April had gone from barely knowing this man to not wanting to leave him. Not because he had rescued her but because of *why* he'd rescued her. The honor and integrity that ran through his heart and soul, the dedication and loyalty he'd shown to his father, to his friends, to his job.

She stroked his cheek with the back of her hand, feeling the coarseness of the stubble on his face. "And you're not bad to look at, either," she whispered, smiling. "I'll tell you everything when you wake up. All of it. I promise."

April returned to her chair and cracked open the water, downing several sips as she realized how thirsty she truly was. As she set the bottle on the table next to the recliner and covered her legs with the blanket, however, she knew that sleep would be too elusive to bring any real rest. Instead she reached for the tablet of paper and pen Ray had left with her. Letting her mind drift back to the dream, to the field where the shooter had stood over Levon, screaming at her, April began to sketch.

SIXTEEN

Voices penetrated the fog first, soft and comforting sounds that were followed by more businesslike instructions. A third kind of sound followed, a low moan, which Daniel realized came from him. The others were instantly on alert, and a hand closed around his.

"Mr. Rivers?"

"Daniel?"

That was the voice he wanted to hear. "A—" His voice sounded dry and clogged, cracked. Daniel swallowed hard, surprised that his throat was sore. "April?"

"I'm right here." Her voice came from his left, and a soft hand gripped his as Daniel fought to open his eyes.

The man on his right spoke calmly. "Glad to see you awake, Mr. Rivers. Everything looks good, but you'll be groggy for a while. We're going to ease off the pain-killers so you can stay awake, but let us know if the pain is too much. Okay?"

"When can I go home?"

"In a day or so. Let's make sure you're clear of infection and aren't going to reinjure the shoulder. Then we'll talk."

"Soon, though."

The doctor grinned and gestured at April, standing on the opposite side of the bed. "You don't want to stay and we can't get her to leave." He made a note on Daniel's chart, then handed it to a waiting nurse. "I'll be back this afternoon."

As the staff left, the room settled back into a comfortable silence. Daniel wiped one eye, trying to push away the lingering sleepiness.

"Would you like a cloth to wash your face? Might make you feel better."

Daniel looked at her, then squeezed the hand that lay so easily in his. "You didn't leave at all?" She shook her head. "Why did you stay?"

April shrugged, smiling slightly. "Seemed like a good idea at the time."

Daniel laughed, then winced, his free hand pressing against the bandages. "But laughing might not be such a smart plan."

As their laughter faded, April's expression turned tender, and she reached up to touch the bandage. "You took a bullet for me."

He pressed his fingers on top of hers. "And I would again."

After a few moments, she eased away. "Let me get that cloth for you."

Daniel couldn't quite believe she'd stayed, but she had, and continued to do so, sleeping in the recliner when she thought he dozed. The next two days became an unexpected blessing, a respite from the anxiety of the two days before. In the hospital, both felt safe, and as Daniel grew more alert, the April he remembered from his father's barbecue outings returned, a woman whose sharp humor challenged him.

When Daniel made an outrageous pun, April giggled. He'd never heard her giggle before, and the sound charmed his heart. He was also charmed by the fact that she only left his side when the nurses came to care for him or when she had to take care of her own needs. The nurses ordered her the same tray that the cafeteria sent him, and they shared their appreciation— or dislike—of the hospital's cuisine.

April did leave the room when Ray Taylor stopped for a visit, so that the two of them could "talk cop stuff" as she put it, but she returned well before Ray left. This gave her time to tease the stoic sheriff about his dates with her sister June as well as ask a couple of serious questions about the case. Despite her hassles, Ray agreed to take them both home when the doctor released Daniel.

Daniel cherished every moment of the forty-eight-hour paradise. He didn't want it to end. In fact, what Daniel suspected before now reigned before him with an undeniable truth. He wanted to spend the rest of his life having these arguments, these laughs, with April Presley. If she'd only have him.

Tuesday morning, however, everything changed, shortly after the doctor gave him clearance to leave.

"Yo, Deputy!" Kip Redding's voice burst into the room before he did. He shoved open the hospital room door and strode in, his blond hair plastered down by a red baseball cap and his work boots stomping solidly on the tile floor. Charlie and Bobby followed him, standing to either side of the taller man.

Kip snapped his fingers. "What are you doing still in the bed, man? You need to get up and at 'em. There are crooks to catch and villains to vanquish!"

Daniel's spirit leaped, and he pushed himself up a bit in the bed. "Yeah, well, the crooks have started shooting back, friend. I figured this is a good place to stay out of the line of fire. Charlie, I need a hug."

"You got it, baby." Kip's wife plopped down on the edge of the bed and leaned in to give Daniel a gentle squeeze before standing again. "How're you doing? We'd have come before, but with Miss April here, they wouldn't let us in. One visitor at a time."

Kip bounced from one foot to the other, pushed his red cap farther back on his head, then turned a bit more somber. "Seriously, bro, how's the shoulder?"

"Bobby." Daniel greeted his cousin with a handshake. "Glad you could come."

Bobby nodded. "No problem. Glad to see you awake. Like he said, how's the arm?"

Daniel rubbed the dressing on his arm. "Good. Good. The doc says I can leave today. The nurse is coming in a bit to change the bandage to something I can cope with. They want me to take it easy for a few days, leave it in a sling as much as possible. But I can drive, do the job."

Bobby whistled. "Lucky the guy had such bad aim."

Kip slapped the end of the bed. "Yes! Let's be grateful the guy was a lousy shot."

Charlie clucked her tongue at the men. "Can we just be glad Daniel's okay without talking about people getting shot?"

Kip reached over and rubbed Charlie's back affectionately. "Feeling squeamish?"

She punched him playfully. "No. I just would rather focus on the good." She looked back at Daniel. "So you're heading out today? What time?"

Daniel shook his head. "Not sure. Sometime after lunch. They're doing the paperwork now, then they'll come unhook me." He flapped the tube of the remaining IV. "I called Ray and he's going to take April back to Aunt Suke's and me to the house. I can't wait to get in my own shower."

Kip pinched his nose. "I can smell that you need to."

Daniel grinned. "Smart aleck."

Charlie looked around the room. "Where is April?"

"Ladies' room. She'll be back in a minute."

A mischievous look crossed Charlie's face. "So she's really been here the whole time? That's not just a story the nurses told to keep us out?"

"Never left."

Charlie and Kip exchanged glances. "Hmm," said Kip.

"Told you," replied Charlie.

"What?" asked a puzzled Bobby.

Daniel felt heat spread across his cheeks. "Stop it, both of you. We aren't twelve anymore."

Charlie laughed. "Keep telling Kip that. Maybe one day it'll sink in."

Kip thumped the end of the bed again. "Want us to wait and take you home? You gotta be tired of cops and docs."

"I appreciate it, but Ray has some things he wants to go over on the way home."

Charlie sniffed. "Back to work already? Can't Ray give you a day off?"

"Not sure I'd want one till this is over with."

"I hear that," Kip said. "Need to wrap things up so you can get on with life."

"No kidding."

Charlie touched his arm again. "Do you know any of the arrangements yet? Do you need any help with them?"

Daniel looked down at his hands a moment. "Not yet. I called Beck's, but…" He looked up at her. "The coroner hasn't released the body yet. Ray said she was waiting on me to give the word. I'll call her when I get home, ask her to send it to Beck's. Some of the folks from Michigan want to come down and are waiting on word from me. I'll need to give them a couple of days, as well."

Charlie stroked the back of his hand. "You know we're here. You need help? You just ask."

"I know. Thanks."

Behind the three new visitors, the hospital room door opened and April stepped in, a wide smile on her face. "The nurse said you had vis—"

As Daniel watched, April froze, staring at Kip. Her eyes widened, and when her hands began to quiver, she grabbed the door's edge as if to steady herself. Then a forced smile spread over her face, and she looked at Charlie, then Bobby.

"Visitors," she finished, then turned to Charlie again. "Good to see y'all again."

Charlie gave her a quick hug, and April seemed to relax a bit. "Yeah, the last time didn't turn out so well. Maybe someday we can all get together without shots sailing through the air."

"That would be good," Daniel agreed, still watching April with a bit of concern.

Kip tapped Daniel's foot. "Look, we're going to head out. Didn't intend to keep you. Just wanted to check in, make sure you were okay."

"I appreciate it. Made my day. And, yep, you're going to have to put up with me for a long time to come."

"Good." Charlie leaned over and gave Daniel a quick peck on the cheek, then shot a grin at April. "Y'all be good, y'hear?"

As they left, Daniel focused on April. "What's wrong?"

She shook her head, edging toward the door. "Nothing. I think I'm just tired."

"April?"

April held out her hand. "No. I'm fine." She looked down at her hands. "Look, I'm going to pass on the ride with Ray. Aunt Suke said she'd pick me up."

Alarm shot through him. "No, April, you don't need to be on the road, just you and Aunt Suke."

She edged closer to the door, her voice trembling. "It'll be fine. Jeff Gage will meet us at the house. We'll be okay."

"April—"

"I'll see you later. Promise." With that, she yanked open the door and fled.

"April!"

Fear shot through Daniel, and he pushed the blankets off his legs and swung out of bed. He looked at the IV pole, but saw no quick way to disconnect himself. He growled and punched the call button for the nurse, then spotted the pad of paper on the recliner near the bed.

He tilted his head to one side, curious. Last night, when she thought he was sleeping, April had spent hours drawing in the pad, her mouth pursed in concentration. Occasionally she'd closed her eyes as if to relax, then they'd fly open again and she would draw more.

Unwinding the IV's coiled tube, he stepped to the recliner and picked up the pad, flipping it open.

Daniel stared at the drawings, his gut turning to stone. He sank down in the recliner, turning slowly through the pages, but they were all the same.

Silver rainbows. Stylized *O*s that evolved into silver rainbows with one leg shorter than the other. Dozens of silver rainbows.

This time, he couldn't explain it away. This time there was no fuzziness about it being an *A* or an *O* or even a stylized arc. She had remembered clearly now, just as he'd wanted her to. The time in the hospital, the lack of stress, the rest. Her mind had cleared, her memory had returned.

It was Orion's logo, as distinctly as if she'd been copying it from their stationery or plant sign...or the front of Kip Redding's red cap.

"Are you sure about this, Ms. Presley?"

April nodded. "I appreciate this, Jeff. I won't be but a few moments, I promise."

"I'll wait here, then. Keep my eyes peeled for anyone coming up the driveway."

"Thanks."

April got out of the car, then hesitated, looking up at her home. *No, actually, I'm not sure about this. But I have to do it.*

When Aunt Suke had picked her up, April couldn't even begin to express how she felt about seeing Kip in the hospital room. Rage, fear, grief, all had seared through her, leaving her almost speechless. It was as if she'd suddenly relived Friday morning's events, from the moment she'd stepped out of the corn rows and witnessed Levon's murder. The hat, the shirt—just as she remembered them. The face was still fuzzy in her memory, but the accessories were clear. Very clear.

How could a man do that? Destroy lives and act as if nothing's happened? Shoot his best friend, then visit him in the hospital? What kind of monster does that?

Was Kip Redding, terrific father and good friend, really that much of a monster?

April's mind wouldn't accept it. Something wasn't right. She needed more clues.

It was Aunt Suke who had suggested walking through her house might help. Perhaps something there would point either toward Kip more clearly—or away from him altogether.

So here she stood, taking deep breaths. Yellow crime scene tape still crisscrossed the front door, which had been pulled closed, even though the lock had been shattered. She broke the tape and pushed the door open, stepping inside.

Not much had changed since she'd seen it Friday afternoon, following the break-in. April walked around the living room, her heart aching from the destruction. Ray's officers had finished processing her home for evidence, and he had sent a firm that specialized in crime scene cleanups out to survey the situation and give him a bid, but they hadn't actually started the work.

China crunched beneath her feet as she made her way around the room, and April paused occasionally, picking up small, broken bits of her life. The heel of a ceramic shoe her grandmother had given her when April was ten. Her favorite CD, the case snapped in half. A shattered picture of her sisters. June and

Lindsey. A sudden ache for them shot through her, and April wished she *had* let June come home early.

On the back window, the threat to her life still shone bright in the afternoon sun. Beneath it, the crushed lipstick, the color she wore almost every day, smeared the carpet with permanent streaks of reddish-bronze.

The carpet would have to be replaced, the walls painted. A new television. New china. New—

Tears slid from both eyes as the true reason behind her visit hit her. She was here to see if she could, in fact, come home again. Would she ever feel safe here again? Feel as if this were her cozy retreat from the world? Looking around now, April knew the answer.

No. This was now a house of horror for her. A place of terrible memories and suspicion. The surrounding fields would no longer bring her a sense of safety and renewal. Now they were just fields of danger. She'd have to sell it and start over again.

She looked again at the threat and the crushed lipstick underneath. The red smears and dots looked familiar somehow, reminding her of…

A flash of memory crossed her mind. Levon crumpling. Her screaming. The shooter swinging around to face…

Blood. April's mind whirled. *The shooter's face, shirt and hat were splattered with Levon's blood. There would still be traces…blood just doesn't come out that easily…the shirt could be tossed, but the hat…the hat was red, blood might be missed.*

Her mind whipped to that morning. *Did Kip's hat have blood on it?*

"What are you doing here?"

April spun, choking back a scream.

Daniel stood in the doorway, his face a mask of anger. In his free hand, he held the pad she'd drawn on at the hospital. "Do you have any idea how dangerous being here is?"

"You scared me half to death!"

"Good! You *should* be scared to be here."

"Why? Jeff is right outside."

"He can't be on all sides of the house at once. This is too exposed. Too many windows. Too close to the fields."

"Fine." She marched toward him. "I'm leaving. I'm never coming back here again anyway."

At that, Daniel's scowl deepened and he blocked her path. "What do you mean by that?"

She stared at him. "Do you really think I could come back here to live?" She waved her arm, gesturing at the living room. "You think I could feel safe here ever again?" She shook her head. "No." She started by him again, but he didn't relent.

Instead he held out the pad. "You think it's Kip, don't you?"

April gaped at him. "Don't you?"

Daniel's face darkened. "Is this why you left the hospital when Kip and Charlie showed up? You saw this on his hat?"

April stepped back from him, crossing her arms. "Yes, and more."

"More?"

She felt as if she were going to be sick. "Yes. The hat, and the shirt with the sleeves rolled up, and the way his hair stuck out from under the hat. Blond hair. It all flooded back, and it was too much. I saw so much at once."

Daniel flung the pad across the room, where it hit

the far wall with a heavy *thunk* and slid down behind a table. "You're accusing my best friend of murdering my father! The man came to see me in the hospital, April. You don't do that to a guy you just shot!"

"Don't scream at me! You're the one who wanted me to remember! If you hadn't pushed—" April broke off and shoved by him, dashing down the steps and toward Gage's cruiser, turning only once. "If you think he's innocent, then check his hat for blood!"

"April!"

Ignoring him, she slammed the door and said, "Take me to Aunt Suke's."

"But—"

"Now!"

Nodding, Gage turned the car around and headed out of the driveway.

April didn't look back.

SEVENTEEN

Aunt Suke slid a steaming cup of tea across the table, speaking softly. "Drink this. Chamomile. It'll calm your nerves."

April took the tea but shook her head, which still ached from what felt like unstoppable tears. She sniffed and wiped another salty stream off her cheek. "Nothing is going to help this. He was so angry. He'll never forgive me."

"Baby, you just accused his best friend of killing his father and shooting him."

April slammed a hand down on the table, making her palm burn. "But I didn't mean to! He wanted me to remember. He begged me to remember. He's been dragging me all over the county so I'd remember. And when I do, he goes nuts. That's not fair!"

Aunt Suke sat across the broad kitchen table with her own cup of tea. "It's also not fair that what you remembered points to only five or six men in the area, including Kip Redding."

April's grief closed in and she crossed her arms over her stomach. "I'm losing him. I don't want to lose him."

Aunt Suke shook her head. "Listen to me. Daniel

Rivers has fallen hard for you. Part of his anger is because this is coming from you. He wants you to be a part of his life, his world. And in that world he loves Kip Redding like a brother. He'd do anything for him."

April shook her head again. "Then it doesn't make sense. If there are other guys who have that cap, then why would he automatically assume I meant Kip?"

Aunt Suke sipped her tea. "Because Daniel is a good cop with a quick mind." She set down her cup. "Orion Materials was located way over in Sumner County, on the other side of Portland. Because of the distance, only a few men from around here went that far for jobs. It didn't take long for Daniel to realize that of that half dozen or so, Kip is the only one who would know when and where Levon would be working that field, the only one besides you who might know about Levon bringing an unlicensed, unregistered green truck back from Kentucky."

April squeezed her cup as if to draw some comfort from its heat. "But Kip doesn't make any sense! Why would he kill Levon? What possible reason could he have for killing his best friend's dad? Especially if he was trying to stay out of trouble?"

Aunt Suke stared into her cup, one strand of white hair falling forward over her cheek, her face drawn, making her look even older than her years. When she spoke, her voice dropped to a raspy whisper. "In this case, understanding the why is a lot easier than the who."

April's stomach clenched. "You know, don't you? You know why Levon died. Why haven't you said something?"

The older woman took a deep breath, lifting her

head. Her eyes shone wetly. "Because I didn't really know anything. Not at first. Because I made a bad assumption about what I'd seen."

April scowled. "What did you see?"

"Strange activity in the middle of the night. People I didn't recognize wandering the field during the day when Levon was at church or at the ball field. But that kind of thing has been going on for years! Kids, mostly. Trying to find privacy for some time alone, away from their parents. The cornfield has always been a good place for couples to hang out. They couldn't be seen from the road, but I could spot them from upstairs. And hear their music. That's all I thought it was. I did tell Levon, warned him that if something happened to one of the kids, he could be held responsible."

"What did he say?"

"He was like me. He said not to worry about it. It never occurred to either of us that something might be seriously wrong. Not even when it got worse than ever this summer."

"How long has it been going on this summer?"

Aunt Suke shifted uncomfortably in her chair. "Since the corn got high enough to hide a car. Maybe a little before. I had no idea what it really was."

The combination of grief, dread and fear made April's mind swirl dizzily. "And now?"

Aunt Suke's face seemed to drain of all remaining color. "This afternoon..." Her voice faltered, and she swallowed hard. "This afternoon Polly brought me something from out of the cornfield."

Aunt Suke pulled a napkin from the middle of the table and wiped her face. She stood and tossed it into the trash, then motioned for April to follow. "Come with me. I'll show you."

Daniel stood over the crime scene, suddenly wishing it would rain. Torrents of it. Streams and rivers and…anything that would wash away the red stain near his feet. Anything that would dissolve his father's blood into the land he loved so much.

Standing in the middle of the field, Daniel prayed. Aloud, his voice choked with sorrow. "Lord, I don't want it to be Kip. My father's gone. Please don't let this take my best friend away from me. Show me what he was trying to tell me. Show me how to reach April. You know I love her. Help me make this right."

With a groan of anguish, Daniel Rivers dropped to his knees in the furrows of his father's field.

"Marijuana? Are you serious?"

"More than you know." Aunt Suke pointed out the window toward Levon's remaining corn. "Used to be, the pot growers hid it deep in the woods. Harder to find on foot, and no department around here had the money, dogs or manpower to hunt for it. Now the Drug Enforcement Agency searches from the air, using infrared sensors."

"The helicopters I've seen over the fields."

Aunt Suke nodded. "That's how Kip got caught last time. Marijuana has a different infrared signal. It stands out from the trees. But!" She jerked her thumb toward the field for emphasis. "But it has a similar reading to some of the corn hybrids planted around here. And once the corn is up and growing, the farmers don't walk the fields like they used to. Too much land, too dense a crop. So the growers stake the pot plants so they grow along the ground, like a vine."

April understood. "Rendering it invisible to the helicopters."

"And most of the time the farmers never know, unless the DEA finds the plants. A few years back, a man at church had quite a time explaining why they'd found two hundred plants in his fields. Had to hire a lawyer. It was a mess."

"So you think someone had planted pot in Levon's corn."

Another sharp nod. "And when he suddenly decided to plow under half the field for a new summer wheat…"

The full horror hit April in the chest, and her voice cracked. "You think he plowed under thousands of dollars of marijuana!"

"Definitely motive for murder." Aunt Suke seemed to droop a bit. "And you probably don't want to hear this, but…"

April already had a sense of what her friend needed to say, a growing dread tightening around her heart. "I walked that field among the corn. Levon didn't. I did."

Aunt Suke sank down into a chair next to the window. "The man who's trying to kill you may not be after you just because he thinks you saw him shoot Levon."

"He thinks I know where his drugs are."

"And that's the secret he'll kill to protect."

April crossed her arms, trying to fight the fear. *I won't live like this. I won't.* Turning to the window again, she looked out over the corn, realizing for the first time that there was someone in the field, someone kneeling next to Levon's blood.

* * *

Daniel heard the footsteps but didn't turn, half wanting it to be Kip…and not. He wanted it over. The soft words, however, caused him to jerk around.

"Daniel, we have to end this."

He stumbled to his feet, reaching for her. With a deep sigh, she sank into his arms, holding him tight. "I'm sorry. I'm so sorry," she whispered. Pushing back from him, she looked deep into his eyes, her own bright with tears. "I won't live like this. I won't."

He didn't want to let her go. "I'm sorry. I just don't want it to be Kip. I can't—"

She stepped back, clutching his hands, tugging him forward. "Come with me. I want to show you something." She pointed behind her. "In the corn."

"What?"

"Follow me."

He did, and she clung to his hand, speaking low but clearly. "You're going to think I'm an idiot, but try to remember I'm a city girl. Plants weren't my thing until I met Levon."

She cleared her throat as she pushed aside the first stalk and they entered one of the rows. "Every time I walked through here, I walked with my head up. Dodging corn, looking toward where I was going. Not at my feet."

She stopped and turned to face him. "Never at my feet. I never looked down."

Daniel shook his head, confused. "I don't know what—"

"Look down."

He did.

And saw the dark five-leaf plant immediately. To his

trained eye, the five points shone like a star. And he heard Kip's low voice in his ear.

You should have paid more attention to what was growing in your daddy's fields, Daniel.

Daniel dropped to his knees again, this time digging the plant out of the ground. "He tried to tell me." He looked up at her, his face reddening with anger. "Kip tried to tell me!"

"So it's his."

Daniel got to his feet. "Why would he tell me if it were his?"

"Why didn't he tell Ray if it weren't?"

Confusion and disbelief gave way to pain, and Daniel stepped away from her. "I don't know."

"Check his hat for blood, Daniel."

He thrust his hand out at her. "Stop! It can't be him!"

"Daniel—"

"Go back to Aunt Suke's. Stay there! I'll get to the bottom of this!"

Leaving her standing there, Daniel ran, a deep, guttural prayer bubbling within him.

Daniel drove. Just drove, as hard and fast as he dared. He was all the way into Hickman County before he slowed down and his white-knuckled grip eased on the steering wheel. The wound in his shoulder burned like a sharp poker, and a storm of emotions brewed within him, predominated by a grief that had no release.

He hated that he'd yelled at April, and his heart hurt when he thought about the grimace of pain that had struck her face when he'd raised his voice. But she was wrong! She had to be! It couldn't be Kip!

Daniel shook his head once, as if to clear it. It has to be someone else. Has to be. Kip wouldn't do this. Daniel dug deep into his memory. When Orion closed four years ago, six men had been left without jobs. They probably all had hats. Possibly more than one. And hats often got passed around. Fathers to sons or daughters. Garage sales.

Daniel hit the steering wheel. He was grasping at straws, and he knew it. He needed to talk to Kip, just feel things out.

But if April were right, he should tell Ray. Let the investigation take its course.

But if she was wrong, and Ray questioned Kip, his best friendship would be destroyed.

There had to be a way through this.

Hickman County, like Bell County, was quilted with small family farms. Acre upon acre of crops rose and fell alongside the road, silver and shadow in the light of the full moon. Slowing down beside one of the farms, Daniel found the inevitable field road and turned down the narrow lane, shutting off his headlights and letting the cruiser coast to a stop. He cut the engine and got out.

The night, still warm from the sun of a clear day, enveloped him in a moist heat, and Daniel leaned against the car, looking up at a sky that glittered with an endless field of stars. In the distance, frogs and crickets broke the silence, and a whip-poor-will sounded from a nearby stand of trees.

"Lord, I don't want to mess this up. I need help. This cannot be about the woman I love against my best friend. It can't be!"

Daniel crossed his arms and tried to listen, hoping

desperately to hear from God. Instead his mind raced through the years, and scenes from his childhood crowded his mind. He and Kip riding bikes, racing down field roads just like this one, fishing poles balanced precariously over the handlebars. The one street race they'd indulged in. If they had been anywhere but Caralinda that stunt would have left them with a juvenile record. Instead the sheriff had turned both boys over to their parents. Later they both admitted they'd prefer to go to jail than face that wrath again.

Kip had driven him to the recruiting office the day he'd joined the Army and picked him up at Fort Campbell the day he mustered out. Kip had been the one to see him cry when his mom died. Kip had even promised to stay clean and out of trouble after Daniel went into law enforcement.

Daniel rubbed his arm just below the wound, which itched. No, it wasn't serious, but it meant something that Kip had come with Charlie and Bobby to the hospital to make sure he was okay. Didn't it? Would the man who shot him come to see him in the hospital?

Maybe, if the bullet had actually been meant for April. If he'd come to check on a mistake.

Kip wouldn't. There was no way a man could shoot his best friend, then laugh and joke with him at the hospital.

Friends talk.

Daniel straightened up at the thought. That's right. What would be wrong with two friends having a talk? Not about the case, just about life. Life, love and whatever else came up.

Friends talk.

Daniel took a deep breath. "Thanks, Lord."

* * *

Daniel stood in front of Kip and Charlie's back door, looking down at the beige welcome mat. Its bright red cartoon balloons, confetti and WELCOME beckoned visitors inside and deepened Daniel's growing feeling of betrayal. After all, he wasn't really here just to chat with Kip and ask his friend for a personal favor. He intended to look into Kip's face to see if a killer lay beneath the jovial blue eyes.

Eyes normally as welcoming as the playful mat. Then, his eyes truly focusing on the mat's details, Daniel frowned. Something seemed off-kilter about the design, out of balance. What…?

"Daniel!" Charlie called his name even before she jerked open the back door and motioned him in. "Tonight certainly is a men's night at the Redding house." At Daniel's puzzled look, she grinned wider. "Bobby was here for our usual cake and coffee night. You just missed him. How are you? How's your shoulder?"

The back door led into a sunporch filled with plants and an array of rockers and lawn chairs. Just inside the door, a wall rack overflowed with work coveralls, hats, ponchos and a line of grimy work boots lined up underneath, soldiers ready for action.

Kip poked his head around the edge of the door from the main part of the house. "Danny boy! What's happening, Deputy?"

Daniel shrugged his uninjured shoulder. "Not much. I was out on patrol, decided I hadn't seen y'all enough lately, wanted to ask you about something. And say thanks for coming to the hospital to see me."

Charlie tiptoed up and kissed his cheek. "That was nothing, hon. You'd do the same for us."

"How're the kids?"

Charlie grinned. "Good. Aaron's out with his pals, Caylie's in her room, doing who knows what kind of girl stuff. Come in, sit down. Want some coffee?"

Daniel smiled. *Like nothing's happened.* He waved off the coffee. "Too late for caffeine. I'll be headed to bed soon."

Kip sat down at the kitchen table and pushed another chair out with his foot. "Sit, bro. I'm finishing up my last cup with some of Charlie's Coca-Cola cake. Want some?"

Daniel sat. "That sounds pretty good, actually."

Charlie brightened. "You always did like my cake." She cut a piece from a plate on the counter, then plucked a fork from a drawer. "You boys talk. I need to check on Miss Caylie anyway."

Daniel watched Charlie disappear. "You have a good wife, Kip."

Kip sipped his coffee. "One of the best. What about that girl of yours? I thought you were standing guard over her tonight."

Daniel rubbed his jaw, the roughness of his beard reminding him how long his day had been. "Gage is taking the shift tonight. I need to get some rest. This is *wearing* me out, and the painkillers the docs gave me for this shoulder are going to *knock* me out."

"You are looking a little rough around the edges. A night's rest would do you a world of good." Kip pushed away the plate of half-eaten cake. "Now. Ask away. What can I do to help?"

Daniel let out a long, exhausted sigh. They had asked each other that same question hundreds of times over the years, anytime life got tough for one or the other. "I do need a pretty big favor. That's why I'm here."

Kip leaned forward in eagerness, eyes bright, elbows braced on the table. "Name it."

"In a day or two, the coroner will release Dad's body to the funeral home."

"You said you were using Beck's?" The family-owned business in White Hills wasn't the only funeral home in the area, just the oldest and most respected.

Daniel nodded. "The family will start arriving next week, and I don't know where we'll be with the investigation. I need somebody who can be a liaison with the family."

"No problem, bro. Charlie and I will pitch in, whatever you need from us."

Daniel tried to look relieved. "Thanks. I appreciate it." He cleared his throat and stood. "I'd better get out of here. Tell Charlie thanks for the cake."

Kip stood, then glanced at his friend's plate. "Which you didn't eat."

Smiling wryly, Daniel picked up the fork and ate a bite. Swallowing, he said, "Yep, I knew it would be delicious."

Kip came around the edge of the table and grabbed Daniel's arm affectionately as they turned toward the back porch. "You know I loved your daddy like my own, and I sure do miss him. But you're going to get through this. We'll get you through it."

Daniel paused, then decided it was time. He faced Kip. "I know what you were trying to tell me."

Kip sobered immediately, dropping his hand away from Daniel's arm. "What are you going to do?"

"You should have told me sooner. Told Ray."

"And get shot at like you and April? I'm too tied up in this already. Daniel, I have kids."

"But maybe my father would still be alive."

"He knew it was there, Daniel. That's why he was planting the wheat. He could have told Ray, as well. Instead he plowed it under."

Daniel closed his eyes, understanding. "He tried to make it right on his own. Wanting no one to get hurt."

Kip cleared his throat. "That's what Levon was all about. What are you going to do?"

"Whatever I have to."

Kip took a deep breath and stepped back, putting the door frame between them. "Watch your back, then. This isn't over yet." Kip closed the door, ending the conversation.

Daniel scowled. *Was that a threat?* As he headed for the porch's door, Daniel took in the line of clothes, boots and hats one more time. Sure enough, there was Kip's Orion hat, silver rainbow and all.

A silver rainbow with a freckling of brownish-red dots across it.

Daniel's throat tightened, and by sheer force of will, he kept moving, ignoring the tight fist that suddenly clenched his heart. In less than a second, his world had shifted once again, from confusion to total chaos.

Daniel looked down, pausing at the door. This was now beyond his and April's suspicion. The hat was evidence. He'd have to call Ray.

His frown deepened, his gaze focusing on the mat at his feet. When he did, what had seemed odd about the mat fell into place, and his lips tightened into a thin line as he returned to the cruiser.

Among the square dots of cartoon confetti, a dark smear had trailed toward the door. Not blood. Instead it was a deep red tinged with bronze. Not a color that ever would appear in nature, but one he'd been staring at for almost a week now.

His best friend's eyes had remained clear and happy, friendly and warm. Yet his best friend had a hat spattered with blood and a welcome mat with a smear of April Presley's lipstick on it. Lipstick probably picked up on one of those well-worn work boots when it had crushed a tube underfoot at April's house.

His eyes burning and his hands tight on the wheel, Daniel drove toward the Caralinda crossroads, turning off on his father's field road, driving deep among the remaining cornstalks. Cutting the engine, he sat in the darkness and took several deep breaths to clear his mind. Finally he picked up his cell phone. He didn't want this on the airways. Ray would need a warrant, and given how news traveled in Bell County, he'd have to move quickly.

EIGHTEEN

Restless, April wanted to do just about anything but what she needed to, which was sleep. The past two days had drained the last of her physical resources and left her emotions in shreds. She wanted to pace, to call June and vent, to bounce ideas around with Daniel.

Daniel.

April sighed, looking out the window and down in the front driveway, where Jeff Gage kept watch. She knew Daniel needed a break, needed sleep, but she really wished the officer in the car was the man she'd come to depend on.

April still remembered the grief that had marred his face when he'd first showed at Aunt Suke's, devastated by his father's death. Her initial confusion after the shooting must have made him think she had lost her mind. But he'd stuck with her, and she knew now it was as much about her as it was his father's murder.

This case had brought out the best and worst in him. She'd watched his mind work through the convoluted details of the case as if he were putting together a 3-D jigsaw puzzle. He'd lost his temper a lot and fought grief, but had also stayed with her, steadying her, pushing her to remember, all the while knowing that the killer had to be local, had to be someone he knew. Maybe even someone he cared about.

But not this. Not Kip.

Emotionally, this had turned into the "perfect storm" for Daniel. His father's murder witnessed by a woman he cared about and possibly committed by his best friend.

"He must not know where to turn."

Outside, the wind picked up, swirling the branches of the trees into a wide arc that scraped hard against each other and the sides of the old mansion. Moonlight danced amongst the shadows and reflected off mounds of clouds gathering on the western horizon.

"Looks like we're in for a storm of the natural kind," April whispered.

She released the tieback and let the drapes fall shut. As the darkness closed over the room, she sat on the edge of the bed, weariness shrouding her. She took a deep breath and released it slowly, seeking her way through the feelings of being lost and alone.

"Lord, I love You." The words burst into her mind, and she whispered them twice. "You stayed with me when everyone else walked away. Thank You for all You have done for me." She paused and took another deep breath. "Now, about Daniel..."

Daniel listened closely, impatient and half expecting Ray Taylor to read him the riot act about overstepping his boundaries. Instead the former Marine's firm voice remained calm, carefully and evenly repeating each detail that Daniel gave him.

"The warrant should include the outbuildings. The

green truck is probably there. Kip must have known when my father planned to bring the truck down from Kentucky."

"Got it. I'm going to call Judge Kitchen. He's a night owl. Is there anything else?"

"Yeah. Pray Charlie's not involved. The kids will need her."

"Already done."

"And, um, Sheriff. I know that I—"

"Later, Rivers. Stick to your priorities."

Daniel didn't know whether to feel relieved or scolded. "Yes, sir."

"I'll call you. Till then sit tight and try to get some of that rest you promised me you'd get."

The connection ended before Daniel could reply. He dropped the phone on the seat next to him, then rubbed his aching shoulder, kneading the muscles around the wound carefully. His gaze drifted over the brightly moonlit field, and his mind remained wrapped around memories of his father, of Kip…and of April.

He'd promised Ray that he'd head for home, try to sleep. No way now. Instead he turned the radio down, closed his eyes and prayed.

April ended her prayer with a quiet "Amen," then slipped between the cool sheets of her bed. Despite everything that had happened, she felt safe in this house, almost as if it were her home. Any longing for her little cottage had eased away, and she knew that she'd be hard-pressed to clean it up even to make it sellable.

Yet one more thing that the killer had taken away from her.

"Help us all," she prayed, one more time, then sleep

took her into a restless dream of this house, the Stockard mansion.

Night suddenly became day in her dream, and bright golden light shone through every window. April darted from room to room in a panic. In each room, she desperately searched for something, prowling through drawers and closets. She had no idea what she searched for, yet she still looked, flipping through books and turning back counterpanes.

When she reached the front parlor, Polly joined her, barking frantically. April ignored her, still pawing through drawers. Finally she paused, puzzled. She stared at the dog, whose barks had increased in anxiety, wondering why they sounded so far away when Polly stood no more than a few feet from her.

"What's wrong, girl?" She reached for the white shepherd, but Polly turned and ran, her barks echoing around the room. April stared at her. Now the dog was running away, but her barks sounded closer.

Really close.

April's eyes snapped open as the dream disappeared like mist before a fan. The barking, however, continued, and she struggled to sit up.

That's when she smelled the smoke.

Daniel almost didn't hear the call, but Martha's nasal voice, no matter how muted, cut through the fog he'd drifted into. Slapping at the radio volume just as she repeated the call, Daniel felt ice slip through his veins. Fire. At the Stockard mansion.

He snapped straight in the seat and reached for the keys. He had to get there. They'd be forced out into the yard...where they would be clear and ideal targets.

Gunning the cruiser's engine, Daniel swung the powerful car into a tight arc, plowing down cornstalks and spraying dirt into a furious cloud. The distance to the mansion passed under the wheels in seconds, and Daniel didn't breathe the entire way. Once he saw the flames, a scream burst from him as the cruiser slid to a halt and he leaped from the door.

Jeff Gage's empty cruiser also stood with one door wide-open, and Daniel could see that he'd crashed through the front door of the house. Acrid smoke billowed out of two broken upstairs windows, and orange flames danced in the window of the front parlor. Polly's barks echoed through the house, and in the distance Daniel could hear the sirens of the fire trucks.

Sprinting up on the porch, he almost collided with Gage, who had bundled Aunt Suke into his arms like a small gray sack.

"Get her into your car and get her out of here! The killer could open fire!"

Gage barely nodded as he looked around Aunt Suke's head to find the edge of the porch and the steps. On the ground, he broke into a run, reaching his cruiser safely. Daniel barely saw him push Aunt Suke into the backseat, but he heard the roar of the cruiser's engine as it sped out of the driveway.

Daniel paused in the foyer, pulling a handkerchief from his pocket and tying it around his face. Heat from the flames in the front parlor seared through the air, and smoke roiled about him. He squinted, trying to see through it and up the long staircase on his left.

"April!" Daniel's scream sounded flat, dampened by the smoke, but Polly's barks intensified. They came from the kitchen, and Daniel headed down the hall toward the back of the house, bumping into a side table as he went. He burst into the large room and realized Polly's frantic barks were coming from the pantry.

Staring through the smoke, he saw a firefighter in full gear and protective mask carrying a woman out the back door. Daniel felt a flash of relief before realizing that the sirens in the distance meant the fire truck of the Caralinda's volunteer fire brigade had not arrived yet.

Kip. Kip volunteers.

Polly's barks turned to wild yaps, piercing his senses. Daniel reached for the door of the pantry and yanked it open. "Get 'em."

He barely got the door open before Polly raced out and across the yard, a white streak that reached the two figures as they stepped over the edge of the cornfield. She launched herself high, a 120-pound ball of anger hitting the man square in the back.

Both figures fell and tumbled, the man cursing and screaming, the woman rolling limply.

"April!" Daniel followed Polly's path across the broad yard, feet digging into the ground as he sprinted toward the fallen pair. Although he focused on April, he saw Polly digging her teeth into the firefighter's arm, then the man punching Polly in the throat. The dog yelped and leaped away from him, gagging.

"April!" Daniel reached her, rolling her over.

Her eyelids fluttered, and she coughed, her fingers clutching as his sleeve. Her voice rasped out the words slowly. "Daniel. I'm okay. Get him." Her eyes cut to the side, and Daniel realized that Polly still fought to recover as the man struggled to his feet and pushed in between the tall stalks of corn.

He looked down at April again, torn, but she pushed at him. "Go!"

Daniel went to Polly, who let out a hacking cough, which evolved into a growl. He grabbed her collar just as she started after the fleeing man.

"No!" he ordered. Polly froze, then looked at him. He pointed at April. "Guard! Guard April!"

The shepherd hesitated, then gave another hacking cough. Daniel repeated the command, then released the dog's collar. Polly broke into a trot toward April, and Daniel snatched the handkerchief from his face and headed into the cornfield, gun drawn.

He moved slowly, trying to listen for movement, and hoping that the man wouldn't circle back around to the house and try to blend in with the rest of the fire brigade. Polly's presence would most likely prevent that if he tried.

Daniel shook his head to clear it. *Focus, Rivers, on what is, not what-ifs. You can't see, so listen.*

At first Daniel could hear only the sirens, but as the fire team and sheriff's cars arrived, they were switched off, replaced by shouts and the rattling of equipment. Then he heard it, the unmistakable rustle of someone moving through the stalks. It moved away from him slightly to the left.

He's trying to reach the field road. Daniel picked up speed but kept his path almost straight, hoping to flank the villain by paralleling his path through the field.

He also still hoped it wasn't Kip. *Please. Let it be some stranger.*

Focus!

The rustling grew louder, still to his left and moving fast. Daniel picked up his speed, knowing they were almost to the field road. In the bright moonlight he could see the land opening up ahead, and only a few yards later he emerged from the corn and swung left.

The firefighter stood next to the dark green truck, a pistol braced in both hands, pointing at Daniel. Daniel dived back into the corn as the gun fired, the report echoing over the field. Scrambling to his feet, Daniel heard the roar of the truck's engine and the thunk of the transmission landing in first gear. Fighting the urge to rush the vehicle, Daniel held back, squatting low, several stalks of corn between him and the road.

The truck charged by, fishtailing and throwing dirt into the air. Daniel waited until it had passed, then stepped out, taking careful aim.

The first shot hit the right rear tire; the second hit the back window, near the driver's head. As the truck swerved and the rear end skewed left, Daniel's third shot hit the front right tire. Skidding wildly, the truck veered again and rocketed off the road into the corn, burying itself up to the axles against a small rise in the ground.

Daniel approached cautiously, calling harshly, "Get out of the truck! Hands up!"

As the swirling dust settled around them, the driver pushed open the door with his foot. Then slowly, upraised hands appeared, followed by the rest of the firefighter. He stood, facing Daniel, back against the open door.

Taking a few steps closer, Daniel ordered, "Take off the mask! Slowly!"

After a moment's hesitation, the firefighter's left hand rose and pulled off the mask.

Daniel froze, his breath locked in his throat as the floppy blond hair of Bobby Martin fell free, framing a face covered in smoke, dust…and fear.

NINETEEN

"Once he got started, I didn't think he'd ever shut up." Ray Taylor's low, even voice cut through the remaining bustle and rattle of the fire team's work. "I let the boys take him for booking because I didn't want to listen to him anymore." He looked around. "Looks like they're about done here."

"Almost," said the man standing next to him, his voice now missing all lightness and humor.

April looked from the smoke-blackened figure of Kip Redding back to the mansion that now felt so much like home. The fire had been isolated to the front parlor and one upper bedroom, and the volunteers had made quick work of the blaze once they'd arrived.

April sat in the back of an ambulance, oxygen mask held to her face and Daniel pressed tightly to her side. She no longer coughed and her breathing had eased, but her chest still felt heavy, and she knew a trip to the hospital lay ahead. The man who now clutched her right hand as if she were about to escape would take no argument on that.

As Ray talked, April stole glances at Daniel, whose face and clothes remained coated in brown and black smudges. The skin around his eyes, white and drawn tight, matched the haunted, grief-stricken look on his face. Finding Bobby Martin behind that mask had been almost as severe a blow as if it had been Kip.

That blond with the floppy hair now stood next to Ray, listening intently and still wearing most of his protective gear. Kip had been instrumental in stopping the fire and saving the Stockard mansion.

Not at all the man I thought was the killer. This was the man Daniel had trusted with his life.

"I'm just sorry it was Bobby." Kip's normal jovial nature had been replaced with a solemn world-weariness.

"I still can't believe he tried to frame you." Daniel's voice, raspy from the smoke and dust, was barely audible. "Or that he almost succeeded, thanks to me."

Ray Taylor shook his head. "No. You were being a good cop. And thorough. You couldn't have known that Bobby had intentionally switched hats with Kip, or that he'd smeared the lipstick on Kip's mat to add to the frame."

As he looked at Kip, however, his frown deepened. "But you're not completely off the hook, Redding. Obstruction is not taken lightly around here."

Kip nodded, as somber as April had ever seen him. "I know, Sheriff. I just hope the judge understands."

"Maybe. I know you had no proof, but you should have told me." Ray's scowl lightened some as he looked at April. "Bobby did plan the frame, and he certainly planned the murder, right down to thinking Levon would be alone and surrounded by nothing but his remaining corn. He didn't count on you, either then—or later. When he saw you staring at Kip's hat in the hospital, then the sketch, he knew he had to do something."

April lowered the oxygen mask. "So it wasn't a crime of passion. Bobby hadn't just discovered Levon had plowed the corn and all of his pot under."

Ray shook his head. "No judge will see it that way. Bobby waited till the day Levon plowed the crop under, and he intentionally set Kip up for the fall. Both actions show premeditation."

Kip stepped closer to the truck. "Well, I for one am glad you *are* a good cop and you just didn't slap the cuffs on me at the first hint of guilt. You waited for evidence."

"Kip, I'm sorry," April whispered.

Kip held up his hand, palm facing her. "No, ma'am. Don't go there. I'm just sorry for what Bobby put you through. You shouldn't have had to deal with this. You did what you thought was right. Both of you did."

Daniel took a deep breath. "Still, I feel as if I should make it up to you somehow."

Suddenly the old Kip was back, and a mischievous grin spread across his filthy face. "You could always make me your best man."

April coughed and put the mask back over her face. Beside her, Daniel straightened. "What did you say?"

Kip's grin broadened and Ray even smiled...a little. "Oh, don't look so surprised, Deputy. Every soul in town who's seen you with her in the last week thinks you're going to pop the question. Charlie's already asked me twice if you've done it yet. Says you look at April the way I look at her."

April felt as if her heart would stop, and she closed her eyes. *This is not happening. Not now.*

"Maybe I should have slapped the cuffs on you earlier."

April squeezed her eyes tighter shut as Kip laughed and bantered back. "Don't tell me you had something big and romantic planned. Let me guess. Candlelight? Roses? A fancy restaurant?"

"A picnic, actually."

April's eyes flew open and the oxygen mask dropped to her lap. She stared at Daniel. "What?"

He shrugged and looked down at their hands, tightening his grip on hers. Looking up briefly at Kip and Ray, he scowled at them. "Get lost."

Chuckling, Kip clapped Ray on the shoulder and the two men moved away, back toward the fire team's cleanup.

April watched them go, then turned back to Daniel, who stared at their hands again.

He tapped the top of her hand with one finger. "I didn't mean… I mean, I wanted to give you more time, but—"

April reached up and pressed her palm against his cheek, pulling his head up. She looked closely into his eyes. "I don't need more time. Do you?"

Hesitantly, he shook his head.

"Then ask me."

A smile slowly crossed his face, lighting up his eyes. "April Presley, will you marry me?"

"Oh, yes," she whispered, then yanked him closer and into a soft, warm, comforting kiss.

TWENTY

Suke Stockard stood at the tall window of the second-story bedroom, looking out at the swirling colors of the late-afternoon sky. "Like God's touch of blessing on this day," she said quietly.

April walked up next to her, the satin of her wedding dress rustling as she moved. "I'm glad you suggested sunset."

"I knew the yard would be glorious."

April agreed, her nervousness about getting married easing some as she looked out over the elegant lawn. As Thanksgiving had approached, the towering two-hundred-year-old oaks and maples gracing Aunt Suke's backyard had exploded with the gold, umber and red leaves of a late Southern autumn.

Having watched the trees turn last fall, April had chosen the red and gold theme of her wedding carefully. Now thanks to June, the yard seemed to overflow with color, and the brilliant reds, oranges, purples and golds of the sky accented the decor.

Dynamic cornucopia decorated the tables and the top of the wedding cake. April had even chosen a modified cornucopia as her wedding bouquet, and the amber-colored horn bristled with bright mums and the fruits of fall. The darker colors made the cream of her satin gown seem to glow in the evening sunlight.

April sighed at the growing number of guests who filled the chairs and loitered under trees. Among them June—who had declined the matron of honor title in lieu of becoming the grand diva of wedding planners— bounced from one group of friends to another. In a gold, wide-brimmed, Southern-belle hat, June looked like a pinball ricocheting off a bright field of obstacles, one to the other, determined to make everything for April's wedding perfect.

She didn't have to worry. What April thought was perfect stood quietly downstairs Daniel and the preacher waited for the clock in the hall to chime the hour. They would emerge, then Aunt Suke and April would follow.

"Levon would have loved this." Aunt Suke's low, husky voice caught in her throat.

April tilted her head, looking closely at her friend's face. "You were in love with him, weren't you?"

Aunt Suke made a soft, derisive sound. "Girl, I've not been in love since Douglas MacArthur left Korea."

April waited, watching as a faint touch of scarlet tinged the older woman's cheeks. "But?"

Aunt Suke slowly smiled. "But he would have done in a pinch."

"Hmm."

Aunt Suke clucked her tongue, then reached up to straighten a section of lace at April's neck. "Hmm nothing, young lady. This is your day, and we're not going to talk about me." She paused and adjusted a mum in the bouquet. "But the man that Levon was gives me a lot of hope about your Daniel. Despite their differences, that apple didn't fall far from the tree."

"He's a good man."

"And he'll have the whole of Caralinda to answer to, if he's not!"

A crisp laugh burst from April. "Hey, he's home folk. I'm still the stranger here."

"Not after this you're not. The people here have watched the two of you. They know you're good for him as much as he is for you. They've fallen in love with you. If he did something to mess this up, he'd be in a world of trouble, with Ray Taylor leading the pack."

Aunt Suke paused. "You once asked me why I stay here when so many have left, when I have no family here."

"And?"

Aunt Suke looked directly into April's face, her blue eyes intense. "No blood family. But sometimes the family you choose is even stronger than the family you were born to. You and Daniel are about to find out exactly how true that is."

Puzzled, April waited as Aunt Suke retrieved an ornately carved wooden box from an antique desk and handed it to her. "My wedding gift. I want you to give this to Daniel tonight, here in this bedroom. Open it together." She paused again. "It's the deed to this house."

Stunned, April stepped back, pushing the box toward Aunt Suke. "This house? Aunt Suke, I can't take this!"

Aunt Suke held her arms wide, refusing to receive the box. "Yes, ma'am, you can, and you will. The deed is already transferred and registered to you and Daniel."

Her voice softened, and she let out a long sigh. "Listen, girl, I'm getting too old to keep it up alone. I've been feeling it for a long time, but the fire really brought it home. If you and Daniel hadn't pitched in to help, we wouldn't have had it ready for the wedding."

She straightened her shoulders again. "This house needs young folks, and I know you love it. So does Daniel. I know you won't sell it to the highest bidder and put in condos. The kitchen and cellar are perfect for that business of yours, and I know you'll keep it at the heart of Caralinda."

Tears stung April's eyes. "We will."

Below them, Aunt Suke's massive grandfather clock chimed, the deep bongs echoing through the old home.

"Time to go, April. Dab your eyes before your mascara runs."

Downstairs, Kip Redding's ever-moving face danced in and out of a dozen grins as he straightened Daniel's tie. "Stop fidgeting, Rivers. We have a few moments. They won't come down right away."

"I still can't believe she said yes."

"Neither can anyone else."

At Daniel's stunned expression, the corner of Kip's mouth twitched again in amusement. "Relax, Deputy, I'm joking."

"Step away, Redding. You don't know any more about tying that than the man in the moon."

Kip stepped back and Ray Taylor, who was standing in as father of the bride, took over.

He focused on the tie. "Truth is, most of us saw this coming long before Levon died."

"Sure did." Kip bounced up on his toes and clapped Daniel on the shoulder. "We all saw the way you looked at her and the way she looked at you when she thought no one was paying attention. Like Charlie said, it was just a matter of time."

Daniel felt a sense of peace settle over him. "You're not kidding? I mean, about the way she looked at me?"

Ray finished with the tie and stepped back, checking his handiwork. "She just needed to get herself together. God brought her here for a reason, and it wasn't to witness a murder. She needed to heal, find Him again. And you."

"How long have y'all been thinking about this?"

Ray looked directly into Daniel's eyes. "Why do you think I agreed to you taking her around town, playing guardian? Against procedure and my better instinct?"

Daniel's mind flashed through all he knew about his boss—the times he'd seen him pray with the men's group, counsel his rookie officers, direct the department with what appeared on the surface to be a military-hardened hand. Hard as nails, with an unshakable faith.

"You knew God would take care of us."

"Believed it with every fiber, Rivers. You have to trust the one in charge. If you can't, get out of the unit."

"Is that marriage advice?"

Ray Taylor finally smiled. "I know you're worried about being good enough, about not disappointing her. Or yourself."

Daniel nodded. "How did you know?"

"Every man's fear, Daniel," Kip said. "I go through it every day, just thinking about Charlie. As old as Adam."

Behind them and up the stairs, the bedroom door opened.

Ray motioned toward the door. "Your girl already

said it. That day on the sidewalk. We're not meant to live in fear. You trust Him, put Him in charge, you'll be okay. Now, march, Rivers. You two have to be outside before they get down here."

By the time the sun's last rays vanished and the red and gold lanterns strung about the yard danced in the evening breeze, Daniel's stomach had stopped twitching, and he'd shook the hands of every man and hugged every woman in Caralinda. In fact, except for the photos, he hadn't seen April since the pastor had pronounced them husband and wife.

Now, as the crowd began to thin out, he searched for her face.

"She's in the house."

He turned, looking down at the white-haired lady in the umber suit. Polly, who had been lurking at the extremities of the yard all afternoon, aloof and on guard, had rejoined the party and stood with her head pressed against Suke Stockard's thigh.

"Aunt Suke. I haven't had a chance to tell you how wonderful you looked today."

She grinned, amused. "Flatterer. Now go. Your bride is in the house, waiting. You're staying here tonight."

Daniel stared at her. "What? I thought we were going to—"

"Canceled. I'm staying with a friend. April will explain everything. Now, go on in, and I'll shoo the rest of these folks back to their own homes."

Daniel leaned over and kissed Aunt Suke on the cheek. "Thank you."

As Daniel closed the back door of the house, the warm darkness of the Stockard mansion felt oddly comforting after the raucous noise of the reception. Daniel left the kitchen and headed down the hall, reluctant to turn on any lights, wanting to savor that peace.

He emerged from the hall and looked toward the stairs. "April?"

A door opened and April moved to the top of the steps, backlit by the lights of the rooms behind her. She wore a soft, silky gown and held a small wooden box in her hands.

"Welcome, my love, to our new life."

* * * * *

Dear Reader,

When Paul exhorts his student Timothy to remember that "God hath not given us the spirit of fear; but of power, and of love, and of a sound mind (2 Tim. 1:7 KJV), he is encouraging the younger man to use those qualities to persevere in his teaching of the gospel, to stand firm in the face of persecution.

When I chose the verse for *Field of Danger*, I did so because it reminds me that while we may not face persecution for our faith these days, we do face trials and troubles that can wear down our spirits and test our beliefs. When life gets tough, fear can make easy answers very tempting.

Staying strong and trusting in God's will for our lives often requires more courage than we think we have. That's when we must remember that such courage comes from the Lord in His gifts to us of power and a strong mind...and most of all, love.

Blessings to you,

Ramona Richards

QUESTIONS FOR DISCUSSION

1. At the heart of *Field of Danger* is April's journey of healing following a harsh divorce and difficult childhood. Have you or someone you cared about had to heal from a time of violence in their lives?

2. Do you think forgiveness plays a major part in healing from such a trauma?

3. It's clear that April has not forgiven either her father or her first husband. How do you think such forgiveness would have aided her healing?

4. How could forgiveness have aided April with her concerns about trusting other men in her life?

5. Do you think April made a good decision in moving to Caralinda to spur her own recovery? In what ways is such a major change beneficial following a time of chaos?

6. In the book, there are several mentions that people experience loss and express grief in widely individual ways. In what ways have you seen those around you express grief? Have you found it difficult to reach out to people who express loss in unexpected ways?

7. After her divorce, April isolated herself in Caralinda, barely interacting with the community. She thought this would aid her healing, but she later realizes this wasn't a good decision. What leads

us to make decisions that steer us off God's path for our lives?

8. Not long after meeting April, Daniel recognizes that this is the woman he'd like to spend his life with, even if she's not ready for another relationship. He decides to wait for her, for God's timing. Waiting for God's work in our lives isn't always easy. What lessons in scripture encourage us to wait, no matter how difficult it is?

9. At one point, April tells Aunt Suke, "At some level, we all want to be needed." How true do you think this statement is?

10. Several times in the book, there's a reference to how the small and simple details in life can help us make it through tough times. Have there been times when taking care of the everyday details helped you cope with larger trials?

11. Other than a death, what events can turn life so upside down that those small details become vital in making it through?

12. When we look closely at our faith, are there simple and practical elements we can cling to in times of chaos?

13. Have you ever shared those elements with others who are struggling with difficult events in their lives? Did you see any indications that your faith helped comfort them?

14. Levon was killed because he tried to handle a difficult situation alone. By plowing under the crop, he thought he was protecting not only his own interests but also the man who wound up killing him. Have you or someone you know tried to solve a problem alone, only to make the situation worse? What steps can you take now to avoid making such mistakes in the future?

15. By the end of the book, April and Daniel realize that they had misjudged Kip. What assumptions about others have led to problems in your life? Are there lessons in scripture to help us avoid making such judgments about people we care about?

Here is an exciting sneak preview of
TWIN TARGETS by Marta Perry,
the first book in the new 6-book
Love Inspired Suspense series
PROTECTING THE WITNESSES
available beginning January 2010.

Deputy U.S. Marshal Micah McGraw forced down the sick feeling in his gut. A law enforcement professional couldn't get emotional about crime victims. He could imagine his police chief father saying the words. Or his FBI agent big brother. They wouldn't let emotion interfere with doing the job.

"Pity." The local police chief grunted.

Natural enough. The chief hadn't known Ruby Maxwell, aka Ruby Summers. He hadn't been the agent charged with relocating her to this supposedly safe environment in a small village in Montana. He didn't have to feel responsible for her death.

"This looks like a professional hit," Chief Burrows said.

"Yeah."

He knew only too well what was in the man's mind. What would a professional hit man be doing in the remote reaches of western Montana? Why would anyone want to kill this seemingly inoffensive waitress?

And most of all, what did the U.S. Marshals Service have to do with it?

All good questions. Unfortunately he couldn't answer any of them. Secrecy was the crucial element that made the Federal Witness Protection Service so successful.

Breach that, and everything that had been gained in the battle against organized crime would be lost.

His cell buzzed and he turned away to answer it. "McGraw."

"You wanted the address for the woman's next of kin?" asked one of his investigators.

"Right." Ruby had a twin sister, he knew. She'd have to be notified. Since she lived back East, at least he wouldn't be the one to do that.

"Jade Summers. Librarian. Current address is 45 Rock Lane, White Rock, Montana."

For an instant Micah froze. "Are you sure of that?"

"'Course I'm sure."

After he hung up, Micah turned to stare once more at the empty shell that had been Ruby Summers. She'd made mistakes in her life, plenty of them, but she'd done the right thing in the end when she'd testified against the mob. She hadn't deserved to end up lifeless on a cold concrete floor.

As for her sister...

What exactly was an Easterner like Jade Summers doing in a small town in Montana? If there was an innocent reason, he couldn't think of it.

Ruby must have tipped her off to her location. That was the only explanation, and the deed violated one of the major principles of witness protection.

Ruby had known the rules. Immediate family could be relocated with her. If they chose not to, no contact was permitted—ever.

Ruby's twin had moved to Montana. White Rock was probably forty miles or so east of Billings. Not exactly around the corner from her sister.

But the fact that she was in Montana had to mean

that they'd been in contact. And that contact just might have led to Ruby's death.

He glanced at his watch. Once his team arrived, he'd get back on the road toward Billings and beyond, to White Rock. To find Jade Summers and get some answers.

Will Micah get to Jade in time to save her
from a similar fate?
Find out in TWIN TARGETS,
available January 2010
from Love Inspired Suspense.

REQUEST YOUR FREE BOOKS!
2 FREE RIVETING INSPIRATIONAL NOVELS
PLUS 2 FREE MYSTERY GIFTS

YES! Please send me 2 FREE Love Inspired® Suspense novels and my 2 FREE mystery gifts (gifts are worth about $10). After receiving them, if I don't wish to receive any more books, I can return the shipping statement marked "cancel". If I don't cancel, I will receive 4 brand-new novels every month and be billed just $4.24 per book in the U.S. or $4.74 per book in Canada. That's a savings of over 20% off the cover price. It's quite a bargain! Shipping and handling is just 50¢ per book.* I understand that accepting the 2 free books and gifts places me under no obligation to buy anything. I can always return a shipment and cancel at any time. Even if I never buy another book, the two free books and gifts are mine to keep forever.

123 IDN EYM2   323 IDN EYNE

Name	(PLEASE PRINT)

Address	Apt. #

City	State/Prov.	Zip/Postal Code

Signature (if under 18, a parent or guardian must sign)

Mail to Steeple Hill Reader Service:
IN U.S.A.: P.O. Box 1867, Buffalo, NY 14240-1867
IN CANADA: P.O. Box 609, Fort Erie, Ontario L2A 5X3

Not valid to current subscribers of Love Inspired Suspense books.

Want to try two free books from another series?
Call 1-800-873-8635 or visit www.morefreebooks.com

* Terms and prices subject to change without notice. Prices do not include applicable taxes. Sales tax applicable in N.Y. Canadian residents will be charged applicable provincial taxes and GST. Offer not valid in Quebec. This offer is limited to one order per household. All orders subject to approval. Credit or debit balances in a customer's account(s) may be offset by any other outstanding balance owed by or to the customer. Please allow 4 to 6 weeks for delivery. Offer available while quantities last.

Your Privacy: Steeple Hill Books is committed to protecting your privacy. Our Privacy Policy is available online at www.SteepleHill.com or upon request from the Reader Service. From time to time we make our lists of customers available to reputable third parties who may have a product or service of interest to you. If you would prefer we not share your name and address, please check here. ☐

LISUS09

Love Inspired

Cheyenne Rhodes has come to Redemption, Oklahoma, to start anew, not to make new friends. But single dad Trace Bowman isn't about to let her hide her heart away. He just needs to convince Cheyenne that Redemption is more than a place to hide—it's also a way to be found....

Look for

Finding Her Way Home

by

Linda Goodnight

REDEMPTION RIVER

Available January wherever books are sold.

Steeple Hill®

LI87571

TITLES AVAILABLE NEXT MONTH

Available December 29, 2009

FINDING HER WAY HOME by Linda Goodnight
Redemption River

She came to Oklahoma to escape her past, but single dad Trace Bowman isn't about to let Cheyenne Rhodes hide her heart away. But will he stand by her when he learns the secret she's running from?

THE DOCTOR'S PERFECT MATCH by Irene Hannon
Lighthouse Lane

Dr. Christopher Morgan is *not* looking for love. Especially with Marci Clay. The physician and the waitress come from two very different worlds. Worlds that are about to collide in faith and love.

HER FOREVER COWBOY by Debra Clopton
Men of Mule Hollow

Mule Hollow, Texas, is chock-full of handsome cowboys. Veterinarian Susan Worth moves in, dreaming of meeting Mr. Right, who most certainly is *not* the gorgeous rescue worker blazing through town…or *is* he?

THE FAMILY NEXT DOOR by Barbara McMahon

Widower Joe Kincaid doesn't want his daughter liking their pretty new neighbor. His little girl's lost too much already. And he doesn't think the city girl will last a month in their small Maine town. But Gillian Parker isn't what he expected.

A SOLDIER'S DEVOTION by Cheryl Wyatt
Wings of Refuge

Pararescue jumper Vince Reardon doesn't want to accept Valentina Russo's heartfelt apologies for wrecking his motorcycle…. Until she shows this soldier what true devotion is really about.

MENDING FENCES by Jenna Mindel

Called home to care for her ailing mother, Laura Toivo finds herself in uncertain territory. With the help of neighbor Jack Stahl, she'll learn that life is all about connections, and that love is the greatest gift.

LICNMBPA1209